Mystery at Bellwood Estate

Best Friends

#11

Mystery at Bellwood Estate

Hilda Stahl

CROSSWAY BOOKS • WHEATON, ILLINOIS
A DIVISION OF GOOD NEWS PUBLISHERS

Mystery at Bellwood Estate.

Copyright © 1993 by Word Spinners, Inc.

Published by Crossway Books, a division of Good News Publishers,
1300 Crescent Street, Wheaton, Illinois 60187.

Cover illustration: Paul Casale

Art Direction/Design: Mark Schramm

First printing, 1993

Printed in the United States of America

Library of Congress Cataloging-in-Publication Data
Stahl, Hilda.
    Mystery at Bellwood Estate / Hilda Stahl.
        p.   cm. — (Best Friends ; #11)
    Summary: The Best Friends—Chelsea, Kathy, Roxie, and
Hannah—try to help Diane Brewster find out who's sneaking into the
Brewster mansion and why.
    [1. Mystery and detective stories.   2. Friendship—Fiction.
3. Christian life—Fiction.]   I. Title.   I. Series: Stahl, Hilda.
Best Friends ; #11.
PZ7.S78244My 1993   [Fic]—dc20   92-41738
ISBN 0-89107-713-8

01	00	99	98	97	96	95	94	93
15	14	13	12	11	10	9	8	7	6	5	4	3	2	1

Contents

1

Kathy's Sad News

Kathy Aber swallowed a sob and took a deep breath. "It's not fair! They knew tonight was our sleepover!" She looked at the Best Friends in Chelsea's bedroom. Hannah Shigwam straddled the desk chair, her arms folded across the back of it. A beaded band across her forehead and tied in the back of her head kept her long black hair out of her eyes and showed she was Ottawa Indian. Chelsea McCrea sat on the floor polishing her toenails a bright pink that looked good even with her red hair and freckles. The strong smell of the polish filled the room. Roxie Shoulders sprawled across the bed with her chin in her hands. She'd wrapped a Band-Aid with hearts all over it around her thumb where she'd accidentally cut herself while she was carving a kitten out of wood.

Kathy brushed back her blonde curls, then leaned against the closed closet door and pulled her knees to her chin. They all wore jeans and sweaters. A weak sun shone through the window. Last night it had snowed, but most of it had melted during the day. Kathy frowned. "Why do parents sometimes think our plans aren't as important as theirs?"

Hannah bent down and patted Kathy's arm. "We'll have other sleepovers." Hannah always tried to make peace. She hated arguments and fights.

Roxie frowned and waved the hand with the bandaged thumb. "So, refuse to go! Who are these people anyway?" Roxie had been a Christian the shortest time of the four Best Friends, and she sometimes forgot how important it was to be like Jesus.

"Nora Brewster is an old friend of Mom's." Kathy rubbed the back of her hand on her nose and sniffed. "And Alec Brewster is an old enemy of Dad's."

Hannah's dark eyes sparkled. "Do I feel a mystery?" She loved mysteries!

Chelsea gave Hannah a look that said some things were more important than mysteries—like friends. Chelsea was the reason the Best Friends Club had started. With a flip of her long red hair she turned back to Kathy. "And the girl?"

Kathy rolled her eyes. "I bet I'll have to explain how to say our last name to her. Aber. Some people actually think it's pronounced with a short *a* and a short *e* — Ab-er. So when I tell her it's a long *a* —A-bear—she'll make fun of it."

"Maybe she'll call you *A Teddy Bear*." Roxie

giggled. The others scowled at her, and she looked contrite. "Sorry."

Kathy pushed the sleeves of her red sweater almost to her elbows. "Her name is Diane, and she's eleven—almost a year younger than I am. The Brewsters adopted her several months ago. Mom says Diane has *emotional* problems. Dad says she's probably having a hard time adjusting to being adopted instead of living in foster homes like she has the past four years since her parents gave her up."

"Gave her up!" Hannah cried. "How could they? Why would they?"

Kathy shrugged. "Mom doesn't know. Anyway, Mom says I have to go to keep Diane company while they all get reacquainted."

Chelsea closed her fingernail polish bottle. The smell still hung in the air. "What about Duke and Brody?"

"That's what I asked, but Mom said *I* have to be there too since I'm a girl." Kathy grinned. "So I said Megan's a girl too. And Mom said since she's only four it doesn't count." Kathy spread her hands wide. "So, the whole family's going. Dad's not very happy about it since he knows how Alec Brewster feels about him."

Her eyes sparkling, Hannah leaned forward. "Just why doesn't Alec Brewster like your dad?"

"They're both musicians, but Dad made it and Alec didn't."

Roxie frowned. "So why is your dad even going to see them?"

"Mom wants him to. Besides, Dad says he'll be kind to Alec no matter how Alec feels about him."

Her eyes narrowed, Hannah glanced out the window. "I wish I could go with you. I've always wanted to go inside that mansion."

"What mansion?" Chelsea looked up eagerly. She'd moved from Oklahoma to Middle Lake, Michigan, last spring and didn't know about the area like the other three did.

"The Bellwood Estate," Hannah said in awe. "There's a huge house with at least a million rooms plus a barn, on over fifty acres. The house has been vacant for about five years."

"So the Brewsters bought it and just moved in." Kathy leaned forward. "They lived near Port Huron the last ten years, but after they adopted Diane they decided to move here where they'd both grown up."

"See if we can all go visit Diane sometime," Hannah said excitedly.

Kathy nodded. "I'll ask. I sure wish you could *this* time."

Roxie jumped up and sat on the edge of the bed. "We drove past there last month, and I saw a lot of horses around the barn. Do they belong to the Brewsters?" Roxie had loved horses all her life and had finally gotten to ride all she wanted when her family went on a vacation to the Flying W Ranch in Wyoming.

Kathy shook her head. "A man rents the barn and pastureland and boards horses there."

Just then the phone rang, and everybody jumped, then giggled.

"Answer it, Hannah, since you're right there." Chelsea was the only Best Friend with a phone in her bedroom.

Hannah reached back and picked up the receiver. "Hello. You've reached Chelsea McCrea's residence. She's unable to come to the phone at this time, but if you'll leave your name and address and a short message at the sound of the beep, she'll be glad to return your call." Hannah held back a giggle while the others laughed. "Beeeeep."

"This is Ty Wilton. I called to talk to Kathy Aber."

Hannah gasped and almost dropped the receiver. She clamped her hand over the mouthpiece and whispered, "Kathy, it's Ty Wilton!"

Kathy scowled. "Not again! He keeps calling me!" She jumped up and grabbed the receiver. Anger rushed through her, but she didn't want it to show. Besides, how could she really get angry at a boy for loving her so much? "Ty, how come you're calling me here?"

"Your brother said you were there."

"Hang up on him," Roxie whispered.

Chelsea shook Kathy's arm. "Tell him to get lost."

Kathy jerked away from Chelsea. "Ty, I'm really busy."

"Don't hang up! Please! I have something important to tell you."

"You always say that." Kathy rolled her eyes. "What is it this time?"

"It's really important." Ty was quiet a long time. "I want you to stop going with Roy Marks."

"I'm not *going* with him. We're friends."

"You ate lunch with him today."

"So? He and I are friends." Kathy twisted the phone cord. "I have to go."

"No! Don't hang up yet. Kathy, why don't you like me anymore? I know I'm the best guy in all of Middle Lake Middle School. You can't do better than me."

Kathy groaned. He'd said the same thing to her yesterday when he'd stopped her in the hall. "I'm hanging up, Ty. I really am." But she didn't make a move to hang up.

"I love you, Kathy. Really love you! It's not a kid's love, but a real and honest and mature love. When we're old enough I want to marry you."

Kathy's face turned as white as the phone. "Don't say that! Now, hang up right now!"

Chelsea nudged Kathy. "Hang up!"

"Who's that with you, Kathy?" Ty asked sharply.

"My friends."

"Who?"

"Chelsea, Roxie, and Hannah."

"I don't want you being friends with them. They hate me. They turned you against me."

"Stop it, Ty! I told you, I can't go with anyone yet."

Roxie grabbed the receiver from Kathy and slammed it back in place. Roxie had given up her love for Roy because of Kathy. Roy had loved Kathy since kindergarten.

Kathy glared at Roxie. "Why'd you do that?"

Roxie shook her finger at Kathy. "Why do you even talk to him? You've got Roy, and he's a whole lot better!"

The phone rang again, and Chelsea snatched it up. "Hello."

"Can I talk to Kathy?"

Her eyes snapping, Chelsea pushed the receiver at Kathy. "It's Ty again."

Roxie jerked Kathy away before she could take the phone. "Tell him to drop dead!" Roxie shouted.

Hannah gasped. "Roxie, don't even say that!"

Roxie flushed. She knew better, but the words had just popped out. Abruptly she released Kathy. "Oh, talk to him if you insist!"

Kathy tugged her sweater back in place, took a deep steadying breath, and said, "Ty, please hang up. I have to go home."

"Then I'll call you there."

"I'm going away—our whole family is."

"Where?" he asked sharply.

"Only to Bellwood Estate just outside of town."

"Then I'll call you there."

"No way!"

"Oh, all right! I'll call you when you get home."

"It'll be late, and I'm not allowed calls after 9:30."

"Then I'll call you early in the morning."

"No! I want to sleep in. Besides I have a *King's Kid* job tomorrow."

"Hang up!" Chelsea said in a low, tight voice.

Kathy shrugged and looked helpless. He really did love her—she just knew it. She couldn't be mean to him.

"Where's your job?" Ty asked.

"I can't tell you. I'm not allowed to have visitors or take calls when I'm working. That's two of the rules."

"Who made the rules?"

"Chelsea. She started *King's Kids*."

"Tell her to make new ones! I'll call you anyway."

Kathy sighed. "Ty, please let me go. I have to say good-bye and get going."

"I'll ride over to Chelsea's and ride home with you."

"You live too far away. I have to leave soon."

Roxie pushed her head close to Kathy's and shouted into the mouthpiece, "Hang up!"

Impatiently Kathy pushed Roxie away.

"Hang up," Chelsea and Hannah whispered.

Kathy rolled her eyes. "Bye, Ty. Have a nice weekend."

"Don't hang up!"

"I must. Bye. I'm hanging up." Kathy waited. "I am!" He didn't speak, and finally she hung up. Weakly she sank against Chelsea's desk. "He can't take no for an answer."

"Because you don't say it firm enough," Roxie snapped.

Kathy scowled at Roxie.

"He probably thinks you're playing hard to get," Chelsea said gently. "You have to say it firmer."

"That's right." Hannah nodded. "You sure don't want him calling you and following you forever."

"He won't." Kathy picked up her winter jacket.

Hannah jumped up. "I saw this thing on TV about stalkers. They never take no for an answer. They follow their victims everywhere! They even *kill* them!"

"Hannah!" Chelsea cried in alarm.

"Ty isn't that bad!" Kathy flushed. "He loves me. What can I say?"

"I know what I'd say," Roxie said grimly.

Kathy slipped on her jacket and zipped it up. "I gotta go. See you girls tomorrow at 10:30." They were all working on the same job tomorrow—cleaning a basement for Abe Parker. "Bye!"

"Have fun at the Brewsters," they all said.

Kathy hurried down the stairs and outdoors to her bike. Cold wind blew against her as she pedaled out of the subdivision, The Ravines, where the Best Friends lived and onto Kennedy Street where she'd lived all her life.

Would Ty call her again? Her stomach knotted. Hannah wasn't right about him, was she?

2

Diane Brewster

Diane huddled in the corner of her big walk-in closet and sobbed into her hands. She didn't want to meet anyone—especially not the Abers, people the Brewsters had known before they'd adopted her. They'd ask all kinds of questions. The girl, Kathy, would probably want to talk to her alone to get all the information she could.

"I won't talk to her," Diane whispered brokenly. She'd stay hidden; then she wouldn't have to face anyone. Kathy Aber was probably just like all the others and would want to know all the terrible details about her parents' death. It had been gruesome and in the news a long time, so everyone wanted to hear more about it.

Diane shuddered and tried not to think back, but the thoughts came anyway. She remembered one day in one of her foster homes.

Anna Colridge had said, "I know why Eve and Leon Atlas died." Dressed alike in blue shorts and white T-shirts, Diane and Anna were both eight. They were in the backyard standing under a big tree for shade from the hot summer sun.

Diane had started to cry. "They were missionaries. The South American Indians killed them! *I* didn't!"

"I know the truth, Diane Atlas," Anna had said in her smug, ugly way.

Diane shook her head. "I won't listen to you!" Diane covered her ears with her hands and closed her eyes so tight they hurt.

Anna leaped on Diane and wrestled her to the ground, straddled her, and pulled her hands away. "Now you'll listen!"

"I won't! I won't! I won't!"

Anna pushed her face right into Diane's. "It's all your fault your mom and dad died trying to teach them Indians in South America about Jesus. You didn't go with them. You pretended to be sick. And God punished you for that!"

"No!" Diane twisted back and forth, but she couldn't get Anna off her. "I was sick!" But she knew she hadn't been. She wanted to stay home to play with Elisa, the housekeeper's daughter.

Anna thumped Diane on the head. "God will get even with you! From now on all the bad things that happen to you will be because God is punishing you!"

"No!" Diane had shouted so loudly her throat ached.

Even now the words rang inside Diane's head. She'd known then and she knew now that she was to blame for her mother and father's death.

Weakly Diane leaned her head against the corner of the closet. She was to blame for all the bad things that had happened. Last week she'd told Nora she hadn't broken the plate, but she had. For two days she waited for God to punish her. Finally He did—she fell down the stairs and twisted her knee.

She looked up at the ceiling of the closet. "I'm sorry, God! Don't hurt me anymore!"

She'd said that many times, but He never listened. He just kept on punishing her. If only she could stop telling lies, maybe then He'd stop punishing her!

"I won't lie again. I won't lie again. I won't lie again." The words tore from her until the closet was full of them, but she kept saying them over and over to make herself never lie again.

Finally she stopped. She wiped away her tears and moaned. No matter how many times she said over and over to herself that she wouldn't lie, she kept doing it.

Just then Nora walked into Diane's bedroom and looked around with a slight frown. "Diane? Where are you?"

Diane froze in place. She would not answer! Nora and Alec were nice enough, but she knew they'd never understand her.

Nora rubbed a hand over the flowered bedspread. Tears stung her eyes. She loved Diane, but she couldn't get past the barrier the girl had put up. Nora blinked away the tears. Surely Grace Aber would be able to help with Diane.

Nora took a step toward the closet. She didn't want to force Diane out. "Our guests wiil be here soon, honey. Come on . . ."

Diane bit her lip. Nora was always gentle and kind.

"You'll like them. They're wonderful people."

Diane shook her head.

Nora peeked into the closet where Diane usually sat when she was upset. Her heart aching for Diane, Nora managed to smile. "Diane, Alec's downstairs waiting. You know, he's not really looking forward to seeing the Abers again. He needs us both to be with him."

Diane sighed. For Alec's sake she probably could go down. Awkwardly she pushed herself up and slowly walked into the bright light of her bedroom. Sunlight streamed through the three windows, making the flowered curtains and bedspread look like a real flower garden.

Nora wanted to take Diane in her arms and hold her tight, but she couldn't. She knew Diane would push her away as usual. Diane didn't like to be touched. Smiling, Nora handed Diane the brush from her dresser. "Brush your hair, and we'll go down together."

Diane stood at the mirror and quickly ran a brush through her dark hair. She hated to see herself in the mirror. She was fat, and her nose was too big. But she did have a nice haircut—Nora had seen to that. And her brown eyes were pretty—Alec had said so.

Diane glanced out the window. Someone moved in the backyard near the trees. Her nerves tightened. Was someone trying to break into the house? "Somebody's out there," she whispered.

Nora frowned but looked out anyway. Diane had been seeing things ever since they'd all moved into the Bellwood Estate. "I don't see anyone."

Diane shrugged. "Maybe it was the neighbor's dog." But she knew it hadn't been a dog. It looked like a man, but it could've been a woman.

Nora nodded. "I heard the neighbor kids calling the dog earlier today. Tassel's his name."

"Tassel?" Diane giggled. She liked dogs, and she was glad to get her mind off someone creeping around the place. "What a funny name. I haven't seen it." She walked into the hall and over to the wide stairs with Nora. Music drifted up, and she knew Alec was playing his guitar. He was hardly ever without it.

In the music room Diane plopped onto the black leather chair she always sat on when she listened to Alec. Nora kicked off her shoes, curled up in the corner of the black leather couch, and pulled a green and gold afghan over her. Alec perched on his high stool and played his guitar. His dark hair hung over his forehead and almost invaded his dark eyes. He and Nora had been married ten years and didn't have any kids of their own until they adopted Diane. He taught music at the junior college, and Nora did free-lance computer work at home.

Suddenly Alec stopped and stood his guitar on its stand. "I'm not going to do or say anything to Tommy Aber to embarrass any of us." Alec laughed as he tucked his striped shirt tighter into his jeans. "So relax, both of you."

Giggling, Diane slumped in the chair. "I'm relaxed."

"So am I." Nora closed her eyes and snored.

Alec shook his head. "I give up. You two are impossible." He dropped onto the couch and tickled Nora's feet.

She laughed and kicked him. "We only want you to stop feeling like a failure. You aren't!"

"And I'm not on TV like Tommy Aber either."

"So what?"

Diane watched them through half-closed eyes. She liked the way they teased back and forth. It made her feel good to know they loved each other. Sometimes she wished she could accept them as her mom and dad, but she couldn't—she just couldn't. The only reason she'd agreed to let them adopt her was so she wouldn't have to live in any more foster homes.

Just then something crashed in the kitchen. Diane's heart stood still.

Nora and Alec leaped up. She pushed her feet into her shoes, and they ran for the door.

Diane shivered, then raced after them. No way would she stay behind! She followed them down the wide hall to the kitchen, then stopped close enough to touch them if she wanted. She peeked around Alec. A glass lay shattered on the tile floor. Someone had been in the kitchen! It hadn't been the first time something had happened to make her know someone had come inside. Nora and Alec had said it was only her imagination, but she knew better. Maybe now they'd believe her.

Her brow raised, Nora looked at Alec. "Well?"

"I'll sweep it up."

"I didn't mean that!" Nora caught his arm before he could move. "How'd it happen?"

"We don't believe in ghosts, so it had to be something else," Alec said slowly. "It was probably too close to the edge of the counter, and some movement made it fall. These old houses move, you know."

Diane didn't believe him for a minute, but she didn't say so. It wouldn't do any good. They were obviously determined to not believe someone had come in the house.

Alec got the broom and dustpan and swept up the glass. He poured it into the wastebasket with a clatter. "I'll look around. But I know it happened like I said."

Diane walked slowly to the windows that lined the wall behind the kitchen table. She looked out onto the wide sweep of lawn that was now brown for the winter and to the white barn with the red roof. Had one of the neighbor kids come inside for a drink? She shook her head. They wouldn't step past the barnyard. And they wouldn't talk to her at all—she didn't know why. There were two of them—thirteen-year-old Stuart and twelve-year-old Elaine. Their dad and mom boarded and trained horses. They'd rented the pasture, barn, and pens from the Bellwoods, and they planned to continue to rent from Alec and Nora. Diane knotted her fists. She didn't want the Blacks to rent from them. And she didn't want Stuart and Elaine Black to have free run of the place—not even the barn.

"My apple pie is gone!" Alec turned from the refrigerator with a frown. "Did you hide it, Nora?"

"Not this time. I finally decided you're old enough to choose for yourself what you eat."

Diane stiffened. They'd think she ate it! She did like the individual pies Alec bought once in a while, but she hadn't eaten his. She wanted to turn away, but she couldn't.

Alec closed the refrigerator and strode over to Diane. "Did you eat it?"

She barely shook her head.

"Then who did?"

Diane took a deep breath. "Probably the same person who broke the glass," she said in a tiny voice.

Nora burst out laughing. "She's got you there, Alec."

Alec grinned. "All right . . . All right . . . Maybe I did eat it and forgot I had. It happens to the best of us."

Diane relaxed. They weren't going to question her like her foster parents had until she broke down and said she'd eaten the missing food even though she hadn't. She turned and laughed with Nora and Alec.

Diane looked over her shoulder and out the window. But who had eaten the pie? Who had come inside the house? She trembled.

3

The Visit

Her mouth open and her eyes wide, Kathy stood beside the station wagon on the paved driveway and stared at the house on Bellwood Estate. The late-afternoon sunlight glinted off dozens of windows. "It looks like it's right out of the movies!"

Grinning, Brody nudged Duke. Brody was dark and Duke blond; they both loved sports and music, and they both played guitar. "We could have fun in there."

"I could hide and you'd never find me." Duke jabbed Brody and laughed.

Megan clung to her mom's hand. "I might get lost."

"You won't as long as you stay with us." Mom bent down and kissed Megan's cheek. "There's nothing to fear. You'll like the Brewsters."

Shivering, Megan brushed a strand of hair out of her face. "I'd like 'em better if they had a girl my age."

"Let's go in," Mom said with a wave of her hand.

Kathy hung back. The chilly wind blew against her, and she huddled deeper into her jacket. How she wished she was at the sleepover with the Best Friends, even though the house looked fantastic. The Best Friends would enjoy exploring it. It did seem to have a million rooms, but she knew it didn't. Mom had said it had four bedrooms in both wings—each with a bathroom, a living room upstairs and down, a study, a library upstairs and down, a music room, a utility room, a large dining room, a small dining room, and a kitchen—all of them huge. There was also an attached four-car garage.

A horse whinnied, and Kathy's heart leaped. She looked toward the barn and saw several horses in the white-fenced pens. Maybe Diane would take her to look at the horses before it got dark.

Tommy Aber walked with his family toward the wide front door. He glanced over his shoulder at Kathy looking at the horses. He grinned. "Come on, Kathy."

She jumped in surprise, then ran up the wide sidewalk after her family. Her stomach rumbled hungrily. Would she feel too shy to eat dinner with these people she didn't know?

Tommy stabbed his fingers through his blond hair that he'd once worn in a long ponytail. He'd had it cut a few months ago when he'd received the job as lead musician on a Christian talk show. He said he hadn't been sorry to give up his weird way of dressing and his long hair. He loved his job and enjoyed being called a celebrity.

Brody and Duke ran to be the first to ring the front doorbell. Brody reached it first, but Duke reached around him and pushed it. The clear tone sounded through the heavy door.

Suddenly the door swung open, and Nora Brewster stood there. She wore red slacks and a matching sweater. "Hello, Abers!" She looked past the boys and cried, "Grace! Oh, Grace!"

They clung to each other, saying how good it was to be together again. Grace was short and slightly overweight, and Nora was tall and slender.

Kathy peeked inside the door and into the wide hall. Alec Brewster stood there with a girl Kathy knew must be Diane. She wore baggy jeans and a bright multi-colored, long, loose-fitting shirt.

Finally Alec held his hand out to Tommy. "Good to see you again. Come in out of the cold."

Tommy shook hands with Alec. "This is a beautiful place!"

Alec smiled, then reached back and tugged Diane forward. "I'd like you to meet Diane, our daughter."

Diane forced a smile, but she didn't speak. It seemed like the hallway was full of kids.

Tommy greeted Diane, then turned to the boys. "Alec, you've met Duke. Brody here is our foster son.

And you've met Kathy and Megan. Megan was a baby when we saw you last."

"I'm four." Megan held up four fingers. "And I'm not a baby!"

"I can see that." Alec grinned as he squeezed her hand. He turned to Kathy. "You've grown up too. I know you and Diane will hit it off."

Diane wanted to run and hide, but she didn't.

Kathy wanted to be with the Best Friends, but she smiled. "Hi, Diane."

Finally Nora pulled away from Grace. "Dinner is ready. Let's eat, and then I'll show you through the house."

"It's as beautiful inside as out!" Grace said as she walked with Nora.

Kathy trailed along with the others down the wide hall. She peeked into a dining room with a table bigger than any she'd ever seen before. Nine people would get lost in such a room! She followed the others into a smaller dining room that was set with flowered china plates and a short centerpiece of fall-colored flowers and leaves.

"This is breathtaking!" Grace looked around the room in awe. It was bigger than her dining room and kitchen combined!

"Thanks." Nora was glad Grace liked it. Nora had made enough money by selling several computer programs she'd developed to buy the grand estate. "Sit down, everyone. I'll bring the food right in."

"I'll help." Grace hurried to the kitchen with Nora.

Alec showed the others where to sit, making sure Kathy and Diane were side by side. He was hoping Diane would become friends with Kathy.

Kathy stared down at the plate and absentmindedly counted the flowers around the edge of it. She didn't know what to say to Diane.

With her icy hands locked in her lap, Diane peeked through her lashes at Brody and Duke across from her. They probably thought she was really ugly. They hadn't said a word to her except "hello" when Alec introduced them.

Kathy moved restlessly. Why didn't Diane say something to her? She looked hopefully toward the kitchen door. After a hundred years she saw her mom and Nora come in. Nora was pushing a fancy wooden cart covered with bowls of steaming food, and Mom was carrying a tall pitcher of ice water.

Several minutes later, after Alec asked the blessing on the food, Kathy took a sip of her water to relieve the dryness in her throat. This was going to be a long dinner! She peeked at Alec at the head of the table. Dad sat to his left, and they were talking as if they didn't have any problems between them. She looked at the foot of the table where Mom and Grace were talking more than they were eating.

Megan tugged on Kathy's arm. "Will you cut my meat? Mom won't listen to me."

Kathy sliced the piece of roast beef into bite-sized pieces, then gave Megan a small amount of mashed potatoes and buttered carrots.

Megan frowned and whispered, "You know I don't like carrots."

"But you know you have to eat some anyway."

Diane heard them and frowned. She nudged Kathy in the arm. "Leave her alone." Diane lowered her voice even more. "She doesn't need to eat what she doesn't like."

Scowling, Kathy turned to Diane. "It's a rule we have at our house. We have to eat a little of everything, no matter what."

Diane shrugged. "It's a dumb rule."

Kathy knew no one else could hear the conversation because of the talking and laughter of the others. She could easily say something rude to Diane and no one would hear, but she knew Jesus didn't want her to. She took a deep breath. "I really like your house. I bet you're glad to be here."

Diane pulled away in surprise. She'd expected Kathy to argue back. "It's all right. But somebody sneaks in and out. I don't know who, and Nora and Alec won't believe me." She gasped. Why had she said that? She hadn't planned to tell Kathy anything.

Her eyes wide, Kathy leaned toward Diane. Hannah would love to be here right now! "Maybe I can help you find out who it is."

"Would you do that?" Diane asked in surprise.

"Sure. I'd love to!" Kathy laughed softly. "You should meet one of my best friends—Hannah Shigwam. She'd have a great time solving the mystery. She looks for mysteries to solve all the time."

Before long Kathy and Diane were chattering as if they were old friends. They ate between their conversation but didn't pay much attention to the food. By the time the meal was over they'd made plans to meet upstairs to decide what to do first. After they helped clear the table and do the dishes, they hurried upstairs to Diane's room.

Kathy looked at the king-sized bed, the dresser, chest, small table with two chairs, desk and chair, TV as well as an entire entertainment unit, and humpback trunk. "Diane, this is fantastic! You could live in here and never leave!"

For the first time Diane noticed just how nice her room really was. She'd been too upset about what people were saying about her and about who was coming in and out of the house to really appreciate her room. "It is nice, isn't it?"

"Of course!" Kathy narrowed her eyes. "Are you used to living like this? Is that why you didn't notice your room?"

Diane's eyes filled with sudden tears. Abruptly she turned away so Kathy couldn't see her cry. "I've been scared," she finally managed to say.

"Did you tell Nora and Alec?"

"I tried, but they said it was only my imagination." Diane turned, her face ashen. "But I know it wasn't my imagination! Just today someone broke a glass in the kitchen and ate one of Alec's apple pies."

"No kidding!" Kathy sank to a chair and leaned her elbows on the small round table. A bouquet of bright yellow chrysanthemums stood in the middle of the table.

Diane stood at a window and looked out at the darkness. A light shone from the barn, but that was normal. Finally she turned to face Kathy. "It's too dark to look outdoors. Can you come again tomorrow?"

"Yes!" Kathy remembered her *King's Kid* job, and her face fell. "I just remembered I have to work tomorrow."

"You work? At a job?"

Kathy nodded. She waited until Diane sat at the table with her, then told her about the Best Friends and how Chelsea had started *King's Kids* to earn money.

"Could I join *King's Kids*?"

"You're too far away to work in our area, but you could start a group here."

Diane dejectedly shook her head. "I don't know anybody."

"But you will! You haven't been here long. How about school? Do you know anyone yet?"

Diane shook her head. "I don't know the neighbors either. There are two kids who live across the road and rent from us, but I don't know them—Stuart and Elaine Black."

"I know them! They go to the same church I do."

"Are you sure?"

Kathy nodded. "I think they'd help find whoever's sneaking around your place."

Diane sagged in her chair. "They don't like me. I yelled at them one time."

"I'll talk to them. I'll tell them you want to be friends."

"No, I don't!" With her fists clenched, Diane leaped up. She couldn't have the neighbor kids asking her about her parents or her life! "I just want to get rid of whoever's sneaking around here."

Kathy bit her lip. Diane did have problems just like Mom had said! "So, don't become friends, but at least we can ask them to help solve the mystery."

Diane thought about it a while and finally nodded.

"Can I use your phone to call them?"

"Sure." Diane motioned to her desk. She pulled the phone book out of the desk drawer. "I wrote their number in the back."

"Oh?"

Diane flushed. "I was going to call them and yell at them for trespassing. But I didn't!"

Kathy punched the correct numbers and listened to the ring. She got the answering machine, so she hung up. "Nobody there. I'll call Elaine tomorrow and tell her to come talk to you."

Diane trembled and weakly nodded. She looked toward her door. "We could look through the house in case anyone's hiding inside."

Kathy shivered. "Let's get Brody and Duke to help."

"No! They'll tell Nora and Alec."

"Not if we ask them not to."

"Are you sure?"

Kathy nodded.

Diane considered it a while and finally agreed. "We'll find them downstairs, then start from there."

"Do you have a flashlight?"

"Two of them." Diane pulled two flashlights out of her dresser drawer. "In case the batteries run down in one."

"Oh." Kathy took a deep breath. "Let's go get the boys and start looking."

Diane bit her lip. Were they walking into danger?

4

The Strange Noise

Diane took a deep breath and walked downstairs with Kathy behind her. The smell of roast beef still hung in the air. Laughter and music drifted out from the music room. With butterflies fluttering in her stomach, Diane stopped outside the music room door and turned to Kathy. "I don't want Brody and Duke going with us."

"Are you sure?" Kathy's stomach knotted. "It wouldn't be as scary with them along."

Frowning, Diane stepped closer to Kathy. "If you're scared, don't come with me."

"But I want to go with you." Kathy shivered. "I guess I'm a *little* scared."

"Me too, but I still don't want the boys with us." Diane nervously switched a flashlight from one hand to another. "I don't know why I even told you about my suspicions, but I did, and it's too late to take it back. But I just can't tell the boys."

Kathy shrugged. She couldn't understand Diane at all! "Well then, let's go by ourselves."

Diane breathed a sigh of relief. "There are two flights of stairs—one for each wing, but the upstairs is connected by a living room. The stairs to the unused wing are over here . . ." She led the way to the open staircase as she talked. Two round banisters curved beside the oak steps and rose to a landing above. "We probably won't need the flashlights, but I thought we'd even look under the beds."

Kathy's mouth turned bone-dry. "It's a good thing Roxie's not here. She frightens easily."

After all their talk about the Best Friends Diane felt as if she knew them. "She's the one who liked the boy you like, right?"

"Yes." Kathy wrinkled her nose. "She was really mean to me for a while, but not any longer."

Diane stopped at the top of the stairs. "We haven't used this part of the upstairs yet, but Nora said we will when both their families come for Christmas." Diane sighed. "I hate to think about that!"

"Why?"

Diane opened her mouth to tell about her parents and all the questions everyone asked, then snapped it closed. She wouldn't tell even Kathy! "Never mind. Let's check the rooms."

Kathy gripped her flashlight and waited until Diane clicked on the light before she stepped into the first room. It was a bedroom as large as Diane's, and the furniture was just as beautiful and grand. "It looks empty," Kathy whispered.

Diane dropped to the floor and flashed her light under the bed. There wasn't even a dustball under it. It was almost disappointing. "Nothing," she said as she struggled back to her feet.

Kathy clicked on the closet light. "It's empty." She giggled. "Chelsea could use this closet! She loves clothes!"

Diane caught her reflection in the mirror and made a face. "She's probably not fat like me."

"She's thin like me."

"I hate being fat! I hate it! I hate it!"

"My mom does too. She's always on a diet."

Diane brushed away her tears. "I never noticed your mom was fat. She looked pretty to me."

"She is." Kathy smiled at Diane. "Shall we look in the next room?"

"Let's look in the bathroom first." Diane hesitated, took a deep breath, and stepped into the bathroom. She clicked on the light. She saw someone standing in the room, and she shrieked and jumped back. She bumped into Kathy, sending her sprawling backwards.

Kathy's skin pricked with fear. "What is it?" she cried.

"Someone's in there." Diane's hand shook so hard, she almost dropped the flashlight.

Kathy took a deep breath and stepped toward the bathroom door. "We know you're in there! Come out!"

Diane held her breath and waited for the person she'd seen. But nothing happened. She glanced at Kathy.

"Come out right now!" Kathy took another step toward the bathroom. What if someone leaped out and killed her?

They waited, but no one came out, and they didn't hear a thing. Slowly they walked into the bathroom, saw two people, then leaped back out. They looked at each other, then stepped back into the bathroom with embarrassed laughs. Their reflections flashed back at them—two frightened-looking girls with shaking flashlights. They watched themselves, then looked at each other and burst out laughing.

Kathy leaned weakly against the wall. "I'm glad nobody was in there. What would we have done if someone had been there?"

"Run, I guess." Diane giggled. How glad she was Kathy was with her! "Do you want to keep looking?"

"Sure, but we won't be scared of any more mirrors, right?"

Slowly they walked together down the hall, checking each room. Just as they started into the last room they heard a strange noise. They stopped. Kathy caught Diane's arm and hung on tight. They heard another sound, then felt a blast of cold air.

Diane's heart thundered in her ears, and her legs shook. She would've fallen if Kathy hadn't been holding her.

Chills ran up and down Kathy's spine. This time was someone really in the room? This time would they see more than reflections in the mirror? Should they run downstairs for help? She turned to ask Diane, but she was already shaking her head.

"We can't tell them. They won't believe us. Trust me." Diane took a step forward, tugging Kathy along with her. "Let's check it out."

Step by step they walked into the bedroom. Cold wind fluttered the curtain at one of the windows. Diane gasped in alarm. Kathy ran to the window and looked out. It was possible for someone to climb out on the roof and get away.

Kathy headed for the door. "Let's tell Nora and Alec."

"No!" Her face ashen, Diane ran around Kathy and blocked the door. "I tell you, they won't believe us! They'll think someone forgot to close the window. A woman was here to clean yesterday, and she aired out the house. She could've left it open."

"Do you really believe that?"

Diane shook her head. "But Nora and Alec will. They won't admit someone comes in and out. I told you that!"

"But the window—the noise!"

Diane shrugged. "I've tried. They really won't believe me."

Kathy closed the window, thankful to block out the cold air. "Let's check the room just in case someone opened it to make us think they climbed out . . ."

". . . but are really hiding under the bed," Diane whispered. The dark hairs on the back of her neck stood on end. "We watched the same TV movie, I see."

Kathy giggled nervously.

Together they dropped to the floor and flashed their lights under the bed. A dried oak leaf lay there. Kathy fell back, her hand at her throat. Diane stared at the leaf a long, long time. Someone really had been in the room! She gingerly picked up the leaf, her eyes as wide as the full moon outdoors.

"This is proof." Kathy touched the leaf with an icy finger.

"I had more proof than this before, but they wouldn't believe me." Diane pushed herself up, the leaf in one hand, the flashlight in the other. Trembling, she looked in the closet and the bathroom. "Let's go back to my room. I'll put the leaf in my drawer."

"Why?"

"So *I'll* know this wasn't a dream." Diane made a face and shivered. "Or a nightmare!"

"Maybe Nora and Alec would believe you if I said I did."

"I don't think so."

Slowly Kathy followed Diane through the large upstairs living room to the other wing of bedrooms. Just as they stepped into the hallway Brody and Duke jumped out and yelled, "Boo!"

The girls leaped back and screamed.

Kathy pulled herself together and sprang forward, shaking her flashlight at the boys. "Don't do that!"

Diane hung back, her heart hammering. How could Kathy get over her fright so quickly?

"You okay, Diane?" Brody asked kindly. "We really didn't mean to scare you so much."

Diane's eyes widened. He'd actually apologized!

"Sorry," Duke said softly. "I guess it is pretty scary in such a big house."

Kathy stepped to Diane's side. "Show them what we found under that bed. Come on . . . show them!"

Diane shook her head and hid the leaf behind her back. The phone rang, and she jumped.

"What is it?" the boys asked, both trying to look behind Diane.

She scowled at Kathy. "Why didn't you keep your big mouth shut?"

"Because they might be able to help!" Kathy lifted her chin. "They won't make fun of us. They're my brothers, and they'd help."

Duke frowned. "Help you what?"

Brody looked from Diane to Kathy. "What's going on?"

Just then Nora said on the intercom, "Telephone, Kathy."

"For me. . . ?" Kathy looked at the others as if they knew the answer.

"Get it in my room," Diane said.

Kathy ran down the hall and into Diane's room. She lifted the receiver and hesitantly said, "Hello."

"Hi, Kathy. It's Ty."

Anger rushed through her. "Ty, I told you not to call!"

"I know, but I had to. Are you having a good time? Is it fun being inside that big house?"

Helplessly Kathy sank to the desk chair. What could she say to make Ty leave her alone?

"Kathy? Why aren't you answering me?"

"I'm surprised you called. I don't know what to say."

Ty laughed. "Say you're glad I called."

"Who is it?" Duke asked as he walked into the room.

"Who's with you?" Ty snapped suspiciously.

"My brothers and Diane Brewster." Kathy chewed her bottom lip and looked helplessly at the others. She held her hand over the receiver and whispered, "It's Ty Wilton. I can't believe he called me here."

Brody snatched the phone. "I'll talk to him. Hi, Ty. It's Brody Vangaar. Remember me?"

Ty slammed down the receiver.

Laughing, Brody hung up. "He remembers me all right. He tried to cheat off my math paper, so I let him. Then he found out it was the wrong lesson. I knew it all along." Brody grinned. "He tried to beat me up, but I'm stronger than he is."

Duke turned to Kathy. "How come he called you here?"

Kathy shrugged. He loved her, but she couldn't tell them that.

Relieved they'd forgotten about the leaf, Diane slipped it into her drawer without them noticing. Maybe they wouldn't realize she hadn't told them what she'd suspected.

Just then Nora spoke over the intercom again. "Aber kids, time to go home. Diane, come down to say good-bye."

Diane suddenly wanted to beg Kathy to stay the night, but she forced the invitation back. "Will you come again, Kathy?"

"Sure!" Kathy would've said more, but with her brothers there she didn't.

"How about us?" Brody chuckled. "We promise not to scare you again."

"I don't promise," Duke said with a twinkle in his eye.

Diane giggled. Maybe it wouldn't be so bad to have them help find whoever was invading the house.

"Come stay the night with me sometime," Kathy said as she walked beside Diane down the wide stairs.

Diane's eyes widened. "Really?"

"Sure. You could meet my best friends."

Diane yearned to say yes, but she shook her head. "Maybe someday." But that day wouldn't come. "Thanks anyway."

"Sure." Kathy silently prayed for Diane. What was troubling her so much? It was more than the mystery she was trying to solve. But what was it?

5

The King's Kids *Job*

With the Best Friends standing in shocked silence beside her, Kathy looked around Abe Parker's basement and groaned. Boxes, rags, and old furniture were stacked *everywhere*. The smell of dust and mold filled the room. She sneezed, then sneezed again. Cobwebs covered the ceiling and hung over the small windows, screening out the sunlight just like a muslin curtain would. Slowly she turned to Chelsea. "How could you agree that we'd clean *this*?"

Looking around again, Chelsea flushed. "I didn't think it would be so bad."

Roxie groaned. "This'll take forever! We should get someone else to help."

"How about Diane Brewster?" Hannah asked. Kathy had told them all about Diane. Hannah longed to go to Bellwood Estate and see just what was going on.

"Great! Call her!" Chelsea laughed and nodded.

She wanted to meet Diane as much as Hannah and Roxie did.

Kathy hesitated. Would Diane even want to come? Kathy shrugged. It was worth a try. "I'll ask her."

Kathy ran upstairs and found Mr. Parker drinking a cup of coffee in the kitchen. Sunlight glinted off his bald head. Bushy eyebrows hung out over his steel-blue eyes. He wore a baggy gray sweater over a blue shirt. She almost turned and ran. But Roxie's dad had said Abe Parker was safe to work for, so he had to be. "May I use your phone, please?"

"Sure, but make it quick. I want that basement cleaned yet today, you know." Mr. Parker lifted his big black cup with ABE written across it in bold red letters.

Kathy hurried to the phone on the wall near the door and quickly called Diane. Nora answered, and it took a while for Diane to come to the phone. With her back to Mr. Parker, Kathy took a deep breath and let it out all at once. "Diane, how'd you like to come help us clean this basement I told you about last night? It's too big a job for just the four of us. Want to come?"

Diane's heart leaped. She really wanted to. Then her heart zoomed to her feet. How could she be with four girls without them asking all kinds of questions? "I don't think Nora will let me." The lie hurt, and she almost took it back.

"Sure, she will. But if you think it's too much

work, it's okay. We'll get someone else. We wanted you though."

Diane twisted the phone cord around her finger. "I might be able to come. I don't know if Nora will bring me in."

"She's going to my house today, so she probably would. Ask her, will you?"

Diane was quiet a long time. "I'll ask her."

"Great!" Kathy gave Diane Abe Parker's address. "We'll be here all afternoon. We have a lot to do. My friends are excited about meeting you. They'll want to hear all about the mystery at Bellwood Estate." Kathy sighed. "But we'll be too busy to talk much."

"Then I'll come!" Diane smiled. If they were too busy to talk, they wouldn't have a chance to ask about her parents.

"See you later." Kathy hung up and turned to find Mr. Parker glaring at her. "Is something wrong?"

"I hired you to work, not talk on the phone."

"I know. I'll get right back downstairs."

His eyes mere slits under his hooded brows, he blocked her way. "What's this about a mystery at Bellwood Estate?"

She trembled. What should she say? It really wasn't any of his business. "Why do you ask?"

"I knew the Bellwoods."

"You did?"

"My son Dan was friends with Seth. Dan was there the day young Aaron had the fight with Lindy."

The names spun around inside Kathy's head. She had to get them sorted out in her mind just in case they had anything to do with the mystery—and so she could tell the others. "Who are Seth and Aaron and Lindy?"

Mr. Parker rubbed a hand over his jaw. "Seth and Lindy Bellwood owned Bellwood Estate—inherited it from Seth's parents. Aaron is Seth and Lindy's youngest son. Aaron and Lindy had a real bad fight, and Aaron ran away. Seth and Lindy still hadn't heard from Aaron when they sold and moved away a few years ago."

"That's really sad."

"Sure was. It's not right for families to be on the outs with each other." Mr. Parker pointed at Kathy. "You keep that in mind when you're a teenager. Don't start thinking your folks don't know anything. You remember, they've been livin' longer than you, and they want to help you."

Kathy swallowed hard. It made her feel strange to have Mr. Parker lecture her.

He sighed heavily. "Teenagers would make it a lot easier on themselves if they'd listen. Take Jane's boy—Jane's my youngest daughter—her boy Ty is giving her fits."

Kathy's heart stood still. Ty? Was it possible Ty

Wilton was Mr. Parker's grandson? She said weakly, "Would I know Ty?"

"Could be . . . Ty Wilton . . . Seventh grader in the middle school."

The color drained from Kathy's face. "I do know him."

"He's the star soccer player, so I guess everybody in the school knows him."

"I guess. I've got to get back to work." Kathy hurried to the basement door and rushed down the steps. "Diane is coming," Kathy said breathlessly. With a glance toward the steps, she lowered her voice. "Mr. Parker was really mad that I used the phone. He says he hired us to work, not talk on the phone."

Chelsea flushed so hard, it hid her freckles. "I'm sorry I didn't check the job better. He said it wouldn't take us very long, and I believed him."

Roxie kicked at a box. "Dad said we could trust Abe Parker. Dad should see this!" Roxie waved her arms at the mess around her. "Maybe he doesn't know Mr. Parker as well as he thought."

Kathy licked her dry lips with the tip of her tongue. "You'll never believe what I found out!" She waited until the Best Friends were looking at her. "Mr. Parker is . . . Ty Wilton's grandpa!"

"No!" the girls cried in one voice.

Kathy rubbed her hands up and down the sleeves of her gray sweatshirt. "What'll I do?"

Hannah smiled. "The same as if Ty wasn't related to Mr. Parker—work."

"I guess."

Chelsea looked around helplessly. "We've got to get to work. But where shall we start?"

"By sweeping down the cobwebs." Kathy picked up a broom. If she worked hard and fast, she wouldn't be able to think about Ty.

By the time Kathy had the cobwebs swept away and the girls had started a pile of things for recycling and garbage pick-up, Diane arrived. She wore jeans and a baggy navy-blue sweater with red stripes around the neckline and cuffs. She smelled like cold air.

Her icy hands locked together, Diane stood at the bottom of the steps and looked around. The girls hurried toward her. She trembled and couldn't speak. What a terrible mistake she'd made!

Kathy squeezed Diane's arm. "We're sooo glad you came! Are you ready to work?"

"Sure."

Kathy quickly introduced the Best Friends to Diane.

"I'm sure glad to meet you, Diane!" Hannah's black eyes sparkled. "We can't wait to talk about the mystery at Bellwood Estate."

"It would be fun to see the horses," Roxie said.

"And see the house!" Chelsea laughed breathlessly. "Kathy said you have a closet almost as big as this whole basement."

Giggling, Diane shook her head. "Not quite."

"Help me move this box of magazines," Kathy said as she tried to push it across the floor.

Diane ran to help. The box scraped across the concrete floor, leaving an almost dust-free path.

Suddenly a mouse streaked across the floor and disappeared under a pile of rags. The girls screamed and ran to the middle of the room.

"Let's get out of here!" Roxie cried.

Diane giggled. "It was only a mouse, and not as near as scary as having someone come in your house and break a glass or eat an apple pie."

"I wish I would've been there!" Hannah cried.

Just then Kathy remembered she hadn't told the others what Mr. Parker had said about the Bellwoods. Diane would especially be interested. Maybe Aaron Bellwood had returned to find his parents—maybe that's who was coming in and out of the house. Before Kathy could tell the story, Mr. Parker ran downstairs.

"What was that screaming all about?" he asked gruffly.

Roxie shivered. "We saw a mouse."

Mr. Parker shook his head. "You girls are all bigger than any mouse. Don't let 'em bother you." He looked around and nodded. "Keep up the good work. I'd help, but I'm allergic to dust." He turned, walked slowly up the steps, and closed the door.

Roxie leaned weakly against a support post.

Diane touched Roxie's arm. "You okay?"

"I guess."

"The mouse is probably hiding in its hole by now."

"I know."

The Best Friends clustered around Roxie.

"Is something wrong?" Hannah asked softly.

Kathy frowned. "It's only a mouse."

Roxie flushed. "One time when I was little my cousin Toni held a mouse right up to my face. I was so scared I couldn't scream. She laughed and laughed."

Diane squeezed Roxie's hand. "Nobody'll do that to you again."

"That's right," Hannah and Chelsea said.

Kathy turned away and grinned mischievously. Now she knew what frightened Roxie. Kathy's heart turned over. What was she thinking? She couldn't deliberately frighten Roxie. That would be wrong, and she knew it. Silently she asked Jesus to forgive her, and then she turned to the others. "I'll start taking the stuff for recycling up to the garage. Want to help, Roxie? That way you can get away from the mouse."

Smiling thankfully, Roxie nodded.

Kathy picked up a box and walked up the stairs and out into the garage. Mr. Parker had parked his car in the driveway to leave room for the girls to pile the stuff from the basement so it could be hauled away.

"Pssst, Kathy . . ."

She froze, then slowly turned. Ty stood at the side of the open garage door. She darted a look around for Roxie. She wasn't coming yet. Kathy turned back to Ty and sighed heavily. "What are you doing here?"

"I had to see you."

"Why?"

He slipped into the garage. "Where are the others?"

"In the basement."

"And Grandpa?"

"In the house."

"He'd be mad if he knew I was here. He thinks I should think about my schoolwork instead of girls."

"He's right."

"If you'd go with me, I could think about school again." Ty stuffed his hands into his jacket pockets. "I can't even play soccer like I did before."

"But why not?" He was the top player in seventh grade. He could dribble better than anyone else. His goal was someday to play in the World Cup.

Ty held his hand out. "All I can think about is you."

"Don't say that!"

"But it's true." Ty glanced toward the door that led into the house, then stepped closer to Kathy. "Will you come watch me play at the next game?"

"I don't know."

"I'll play better if you're watching me."

Before she could answer, the door opened and Roxie stepped out with a box in her hands. Ty darted out the garage door.

Roxie set the box down and looked toward the door. Chilly wind blew in. "Who was that?"

"Ty Wilton."

"I can't believe he came when he knew he wasn't supposed to."

Kathy shrugged. Part of her was happy he came and part of her angry. She couldn't understand how she could feel both ways.

"He'd better not come in here while I'm around!" Roxie headed for the door into the house. "Are you coming?"

Kathy shivered and ran after Roxie.

Three hours later Kathy rubbed her tired back, then sat with the Best Friends and Diane at Chelsea's kitchen table. "I hope we never have that hard of a job again."

Roxie drank her soda and set the glass down. "It's a good thing Ty Wilton stayed away from us!"

"He's persistent, isn't he?" Diane folded her hands in her lap. She'd probably go through her entire life without a boy liking her.

Just then Kathy remembered what Mr. Parker had said about the Bellwoods. Her eyes sparkled as she leaned forward. "Wait'll you hear what Mr. Parker told me!" Kathy told the girls, and then leaned back with a smug look on her face. "Aaron Bellwood might be the answer to the mystery. I probably solved it without a big investigation."

Diane shook her head. "It can't be Aaron Bellwood. Alec said the house was put up for sale because the Bellwoods learned their son Aaron was dead."

Kathy sagged in defeat. They were right back where they'd started.

6

The Accident

While the girls talked about the mystery, Diane picked up her glass from the table in Chelsea's kitchen and walked toward the sink. Suddenly she tripped. The glass flew from her hands and smashed against the counter, and she sprawled to the floor. Pain shot through her, and she moaned.

"Diane!" the Best Friends cried as they rushed over to her.

"Are you hurt?" Kathy tried to lift Diane, but she was too heavy.

Tears filled Diane's eyes, and she tried to blink them away. Awkwardly she pushed herself up. Her hands stung from slamming against the floor. Her knees ached, and she rubbed them gingerly.

Hannah gently touched Diane's arm. "Can you stand? Is anything broken?"

Diane brushed back her dark hair and sank to her chair. "Bad things always happen to me!"

"You have angels watching over you." Kathy sat back down as the others did.

Diane shook her head. "Not me. God is mad at me."

The girls gasped.

"He *loves* you!" Hannah reached out for Diane, and then pulled her hand back. She could see Diane didn't want to be touched.

"If He loved me, He wouldn't always be hurting me."

Roxie frowned. She didn't know God would hurt anyone. Was He going to hurt her when she did something wrong?

Chelsea shook her head. "Diane, God doesn't hurt you. The Bible says Jesus came to give abundant life. Satan came to steal, kill, and destroy."

"But what if I sin?"

"You put yourself into Satan's territory so he can hurt you in some way. But *God* doesn't do that."

Hannah added, "And when you sin, you can ask Jesus to forgive you and He will. He doesn't hurt you—He forgives you and helps you live the way He wants you to live."

Diane's heart leaped. Was it possible? She swallowed hard. Dare she ask them an important, very personal question? She licked her lips. "Say somebody told a lie and say it made somebody die. What then?" She held her breath and waited.

Hannah smiled. "That person should ask Jesus to forgive him for telling a lie."

Roxie frowned. "How could a lie make somebody die?"

Diane pulled into herself. "Never mind . . . I was just asking . . . It's not important."

"I think it is," Kathy said softly. "One of the things the Best Friends do for each other is talk about what's bothering them. Then we pray for each other. If something is bothering you, you can tell us. We'll help you, and we'll pray for you."

Diane brushed at her eyes. Could she tell them? Could she finally be free of her terrible guilt?

Just then the phone rang. Chelsea ran to answer it. She talked a while, then held the phone out to Kathy. "It's for you."

Kathy's heart sank. "Ty again?"

Chelsea shook her head. "Your mom."

"It's a good thing." Roxie scowled at the phone. It wasn't fair to Roy for Ty to call Kathy.

Kathy took the receiver. "Hi, Mom. What's up?"

"Nora and I have been talking, and we decided we'd like to go out together tonight—the four of us, Nora and Alec, your dad and me. So I said you'd stay the night with Diane. Is that all right?"

Kathy hesitated a fraction of a second. "Sure. Shouldn't I see if it's okay with her?"

"Yes. Please do."

Holding her hand over the receiver, Kathy turned

to Diane and told her what their moms wanted. "So, would you like me to spend the night?"

"Sure!" Diane smiled. Maybe she'd find the courage to ask Kathy more about angels and God's punishment and Satan's evil work.

"Good." Kathy talked to her mom a couple of minutes more and hung up. "It's all settled."

"I wish we could all spend the night!" Hannah cried.

"I'll ask Nora if you can another night." Diane's eyes sparkled. She'd never met anyone like these four girls before. They were really nice, and they actually liked her. Or did they like her because of the house and the mystery? The sparkle left her eyes, and her shoulders sagged.

An hour later Kathy and Diane stood in Diane's yard and looked toward the barn, then up at the gray sky. Their parents had driven off, saying they'd be home about midnight.

Kathy huddled into her jacket. Cold wind blew against her, and she shivered. She'd called Stuart and Elaine Black a few minutes ago to see if it was all right to look at the horses. They said they'd meet them at the barn. Diane acted like she didn't want to go. "If you don't think we should go to the barn to see the horses, we won't."

Diane shrugged. "It's all right."

Kathy's heart leaped. She'd be within petting distance of a horse!

"But we won't stay long." Diane pushed her icy hands into her jacket pockets. She really didn't want to see Stuart and Elaine, but she knew Kathy wanted to see the horses and the kids. "It'll be dark soon, and I hate to be outdoors after dark. It seems so much darker in the country at night than in town."

Kathy agreed. "Because of no streetlights and houses."

Diane fell into step with Kathy as they hurried across the yard toward the barn. "I didn't know until I moved here that you can't see stars in town. Because of the lights, you know."

"You're right. I never realized that either."

"I love seeing the stars." Diane looked up at the gray sky where not a single star was in sight tonight. "Sometimes they're so close it's like I could touch them."

Just then a golden retriever ran up to the girls. It sniffed them and wagged its tail.

"You must be Tassel." Laughing, Diane patted the dog.

Kathy giggled. "Tassel? Because its tail looks like a tassel?"

"I guess. It's a funny name, isn't it?" Diane pulled a burr off Tassel's coat and dropped it to the ground. "You're a pretty dog. It might be fun to have a dog."

"We can't have one in town. Dad won't allow a dog in the house, and Mom says dogs shouldn't be tied up."

On the other side of the white fence Stuart and Elaine Black waved to the girls. Stuart was in seventh grade and Elaine sixth. The wind tousled Stuart's dark red hair. A bright green hat covered most of Elaine's long brown hair. Their cheeks and noses were red from the cold wind.

Kathy ran to the fence and climbed over. "Hi, Stuart! Hi, Elaine! Is this your dog?"

Stuart nodded.

"That's Tassel," Elaine said as Tassel pushed his nose into her mittened hand.

Diane looked longingly back toward the house. She froze. Had she seen someone walk in the back door? She'd know soon enough. She'd closed the door on a piece of her math homework. If it wasn't in the door when they returned, she'd know someone had opened the door. But if it was there, what then? Would she have to admit she'd been seeing things just like Nora and Alec had said? Impatiently Diane turned away from the house and ran to the fence to join the others.

With Stuart and Elaine beside her, Kathy walked inside the big white barn. The two long rows of stalls on either side of the concrete aisle were full of horses. The barn smelled like horses and hay and felt warm from the animals' body heat. Horses stuck their heads out of the stalls and nickered.

Stuart stopped at the first stall and patted the

white blaze on the black horse's nose. "This is Jagger, and he's ours. We board and train the rest of them."

Elaine darted a look at Diane at the door, then stepped close to Kathy and whispered, "Unless *they* won't rent to us any longer. It was better when the house was empty."

Diane saw Elaine whispering to Kathy, and her mouth turned bone-dry. Was Elaine saying something mean about her?

Stuart motioned to Diane. "Want to see the horses up close? They're real beauties, and they won't hurt you."

Diane hesitantly joined Stuart and walked beside him, with Kathy and Elaine following close behind. Stuart told them the name of each horse and who owned it.

Kathy patted a palomino on the neck. "This is my favorite. Someday I'd like to have a horse just like this. But first I'd have to learn to ride better."

"We give riding lessons too," Elaine said. "Of course, not many now because of the cold weather."

Stuart smiled at Diane. "Do you know how to ride?"

She frowned. Was he making fun of her? How could she have learned how to ride? She barely shook her head.

"It's fun. We'll teach you if you want."

Diane swallowed hard. "The horses are all so tall! Riding seems kind of scary."

"It's not really." Stuart fixed the halter strap on a big bay. "Not when you get used to the horse."

"We've been riding all our lives," Elaine said. "I was bucked off a few times and got scared, but I got over it."

Stuart laughed. "She cried a lot, but Dad helped her until she wasn't afraid any longer."

Just then Diane glanced out the window. Snowflakes danced in the air. "It's snowing! And it's getting dark. We've got to get back to the house, Kathy."

Shivering, Kathy turned to Stuart and Elaine. "We'll see you in church tomorrow."

"See ya," they both said.

Diane patted Tassel one last time, hurried to the fence, and climbed over very carefully. It would be totally embarrassing if she caught her foot and sprawled to the ground while the others were watching.

Kathy easily dropped to the ground and waited for Diane. "Someday I'd like a horse of my own. Roxie got to go to a ranch in Wyoming last summer, and she loved it. Wouldn't that be fun?"

"I'm not really into riding." Diane flushed. If she weren't so fat, she'd love to ride. She ran across the yard with Kathy close beside her.

Wind swirled snow in the darkening sky and rustled dead oak leaves still hanging on the huge trees.

Tassel barked. The smell of wood smoke drifted down and around the yard from the Blacks' house.

At the house Diane reached to open the storm door, hesitated, then opened it. The paper was still in the wooden door where she'd put it. Or had the person who was going in and out of the house seen the paper and put it back when he closed the door?

Kathy looked at Diane questioningly. "What's wrong?" Was Diane going to start acting strange again?

"Nothing." Diane opened the door and caught the paper before it fell. Heat rushed at her, burning her skin. She stepped aside to let Kathy in, then clicked on the light.

Kathy shrugged out of her coat and shook off the snowflakes. She hung the coat in the closet and slipped off her boots. "Want to play Clue now?" Kathy loved playing Clue, and she'd brought her game since Diane didn't have it.

Diane hung her coat, took a deep breath, and faced Kathy. "I want to look through the house again . . . Just to make sure no one is in here."

Kathy shrugged. She didn't really think anyone was in the house, but she wanted Diane to be relaxed enough to play the game.

Several minutes later the girls walked into the last bedroom in the unused wing of the house. Lights blazed from every room they'd already searched. Diane shot the beam from her flashlight under the bed, then inside the corners of the closet. She sighed in relief. "Nobody," she whispered.

"Now can we play Clue?"

"We still have to check all the other rooms."

Kathy sighed heavily but walked along beside Diane. She clicked off each bedroom light as they passed them. Suddenly the lights they hadn't reached yet went out, and they were plunged into darkness. Diane screamed and dropped her flashlight. It rolled away and clunked against the wall. Kathy forced back a scream. Her hand shook so much, she couldn't get her light on. Finally she did, but the light seemed very dim in such darkness.

"Who turned out the lights?" Diane cried as she frantically crawled around looking for her flashlight.

"Maybe the wind blew down a line." Kathy felt Diane's tension, and it made her shiver. What could they do? What if someone was hiding and jumped out and attacked them? She gripped the flashlight. Wait! What was she doing? Fear had no place in her! God was with them! He was always with them, even in the dark! Silently she prayed for help.

Tears streamed down Diane's cheeks. "I can't find my flashlight. I can't find it!"

Trembling, Kathy flashed her light around until finally the beam landed on Diane's flashlight.

Diane sprang forward and clutched the light as if it were her life. She pressed against the wall, the light tight against her chest.

Kathy gently touched Diane's shoulder. "Let's go downstairs. You'll feel better there."

Diane moaned.

"We have angels watching over us, Diane," Kathy said softly. "We don't have to fear."

Diane looked intently at Kathy. "Are you really really sure?"

"The Bible says so, so it's true."

Slowly Diane walked beside Kathy to the stairs and on down. Their footsteps echoed in the house. Wind whistled around the corner of the house and sounded extra-loud.

In the kitchen Kathy stopped beside the counter. "Do you have candles or a kerosene lamp?"

"There are candles up here . . ." Diane lifted one pink candle and its glass holder down from the shelf and set it on the table. She found matches in the drawer where Alec and Nora kept foil and wax paper, then lit the candle. The smell of sulfur stayed in the air a minute, then was gone. The flame glowed brightly a second and flickered down to a tiny light.

Kathy giggled. "We can play Clue by candle-light."

Her eyes wide with horror, Diane turned to face Kathy. "Play? How can you even think about playing at a time like this?"

"Why not? What else can we do? The TV won't work. We can't bake cookies like we'd planned. Clue would be fun to play."

Just then the floor above them creaked.

Diane gasped and stared up at the ceiling.

Kathy swallowed hard. Was someone in the house after all?

7

Snowed In

Kathy caught Diane's icy hand and held it firmly. "Diane, listen to me . . ."

The floor creaked again, and Diane screamed.

Trembling, Kathy squeezed Diane's hand. "Listen to me! Houses creak, especially when the temperature changes. That's what my dad says. Even our house creaks. Please, relax."

Diane whimpered and tried to listen to Kathy.

"A verse in Psalm 91 says that if we live in God, no harm can come to us and no disaster will come near our homes." Kathy quoted more of the verses until Diane finally stopped crying. They sat side by side at the kitchen table with the candle casting a soft light over them. "Diane, why do you think God wants to hurt you?"

Diane tensed. Dare she tell? She took a deep breath and slowly let it out. "This girl I once knew in a foster home told me God punishes people who do wrong. She said He gives them diseases and kills them in car wrecks and things like that."

Kathy shook her head. How could anyone say such a terrible thing? "Why did you believe her?"

Diane's eyes widened. Why had she? "I . . . I don't know."

"Did you ever look in the Bible to find the answer for yourself?"

"I never thought about doing that."

"Did you just take her word for it?"

Diane nodded.

"When someone tells you something that's in the Bible, always check it out for yourself. You need to see with your own eyes what's true and what's not. Where's your Bible?"

Diane shivered. "In my room. But we can't go get it right now."

"Sure, we can." With her flashlight in hand, Kathy jumped up. "Come on."

"No! I just can't! I know somebody's upstairs waiting to hurt us."

"I'll go alone then. You wait right here."

Diane shoved back her chair. "No way! We have to stay together." She caught Kathy's sleeve and stopped her. "Why do you need my Bible?"

"To show you Scriptures that will show you God loves you and protects you and is your helper all the time."

"You don't have to show me now, do you? It can wait until the lights come back on."

Just then the phone rang, shattering the silence of the kitchen. Diane squealed, and Kathy jumped.

"Want me to answer it?" Kathy whispered.

Diane nodded.

Kathy hurried to the desk tucked in the corner with shelves of cookbooks above it. She reached for the phone, then froze. What if it was Ty? He'd know by now she was here—he had a way of learning where she was.

Diane nudged Kathy in the back. "Aren't you going to answer it?"

"Of course." Her mouth dry, Kathy answered.

"Kathy? It's Elaine Black."

"Oh, hi!" Kathy sagged in relief, then whispered who it was to Diane.

"My mom said to call to see if you girls were all right. Our lights are out too, and she thought you might be afraid."

"We're okay. We lit a candle and are in the kitchen."

"Dad called Consumers Power, and they said they were working on the problem. If you get scared, you could come over here and stay with us."

"Let me ask Diane." Kathy held her hand over the mouthpiece. "Elaine's mom says to go over there if we're scared."

Diane shook her head. She couldn't handle going

there where they'd ask her all kinds of questions. "We'll be all right here."

Kathy nodded and told Elaine. "Thanks for calling."

"If you change your mind, come on over."

"We will. Thanks." Slowly Kathy hung up. Immediately the phone rang, shattering the silence again, and she jumped.

"It might be Nora checking on us. I'll get it." Diane reached around Kathy and answered it. It *was* Nora, wanting to know how they were. "We're fine." Diane didn't feel fine, but she wasn't as frightened as she had been a few minutes earlier, thanks to Kathy's comforting words.

"Are you sure? You sound strange."

"No, really, we're all right. We're getting ready to play a game of Clue."

"Have fun."

"Thanks. We will." Diane hung up and sighed heavily. "It was Nora. I was afraid to tell her the lights are out or they'd have worried about us and come home. This was the first night they've gone out without me since they adopted me. I didn't want them to be mad at me for spoiling their night out."

"They were probably so glad to adopt you, they don't care if they ever go out alone."

"Yeah, sure."

"Don't you believe me?"

"Why should I? Just look at me!" Diane thumped her chest. "Who'd want me?"

"They did."

"They probably felt sorry for me."

Kathy frowned. "If they'd adopted someone for that reason, they could've picked someone else. But they chose *you*."

Diane's eyes widened, and her heart jerked strangely. They had picked her! How strange. Why in the world would they take her over someone else—someone cuter and younger? She'd never thought of that before. "I hope they have fun." She waved her hand. "Well, do you want to play Clue or what?"

Kathy laughed. "I sure do! I'll get it!"

Diane caught her arm. "Where is it?"

"Oh, come on! It's on the counter near the back door." Kathy flashed her light in Diane's eyes. "I thought you weren't going to be afraid anymore."

Diane grinned sheepishly. "Sorry."

They played two games, and Diane won them both. Kathy helplessly shook her head. "You're really good at this!"

"Well, it's harder when more than two play. I played it a lot in the last foster home I was in."

"What was it like being in a foster home?"

"Some were okay, and some weren't." Diane shivered. "I'm getting cold."

"I forgot that the furnace doesn't work if the electricity is off." Kathy ran to the closet and pulled out their jackets. She tossed Diane's to her. Kathy started to stick her arms in the sleeves when the lights flashed on, blazing brighter than a summer sun. She blinked and laughed. "Lights again!"

"What a relief," Diane said under her breath. She heard the furnace kick on and the refrigerator start. Once again the house was full of the normal sounds. She remembered the lights she'd left on upstairs in the empty wing. She didn't want Nora and Alec to know she'd been in that part of the house. The last time she'd checked it over for an intruder, they'd told her to stay out of it. They said she was only scaring herself by thinking someone was coming inside the house. Slowly she turned to Kathy. "We have to turn the lights off upstairs."

"Want your flashlight?"

Diane nodded. She hesitated, then told Kathy why she couldn't leave the lights on. "I don't want them mad at me."

Kathy kept one flashlight and gave the other to Diane as they started toward the steps. "I don't like it when my mom and dad get mad at me either. It makes me sad."

"My real mom and dad sometimes got mad at me." Diane almost choked on the words. Why had she brought up her parents?

Kathy stopped and stared in surprise at Diane. "Do you know where they are?"

Diane frowned. "How can you even ask?"

Everyone knew they were in Heaven. Did Kathy think they'd gone to Hell when they died?

Kathy cleared her throat. "Somebody said . . . they gave you away."

"No!" Diane shook her head hard. "They *died*! I stayed home and *they* died!" Her voice rose, and she knew she was shouting, but she couldn't stop herself. Now that she'd started talking about them, it all came pouring out. "I should've been with them, but I wasn't. I stayed home to play with Elisa. I wanted to play with Elisa more than I wanted to go with Momma and Daddy!"

Kathy saw the despair on Diane's face and heard the anguish in her voice. Silently Kathy prayed for the right words to say to her.

With an agonizing wail Diane dropped to the step and pushed her head against the banister.

Kathy sat beside her and put an arm across her shoulders. "You were a little girl. Of course you'd want to play more than go with them. It's all right."

"No!" Diane shook her head hard. "I lied! I said I was sick, and they believed me!"

"Jesus knows you're sorry for telling a lie. He wants you to forgive yourself."

"Forgive myself? I can't!"

"Your mom and dad won't hold it against you. They're in Heaven now, so they would naturally forgive you."

"God is punishing me for that lie!"

"No, Diane. The minute you ask Jesus to forgive you, in God's sight it's totally wiped away as if it never happened. Satan's the one who wants you to remember and be in agony. Satan is our enemy, and he wants to destroy us. But Jesus gave us victory over Satan. The only way he can destroy us is if we let him." Kathy tapped Diane's back. "And you will not let him destroy you! Right?"

Diane slowly lifted her head and wiped off her wet face with a tissue from her pocket. Was Kathy right? "Help me, Kathy. Please."

"Sure, I will!" Kathy smiled even as she prayed for the right words to say. "The most important thing to do is read your Bible so you can really learn what God is like. He loves you!" Kathy talked for a long time until Diane began to understand.

Finally Diane stood and smiled. "I guess we better turn the lights off."

"Let's go." Kathy jumped up and started up the stairs just as the phone rang.

"We don't have a phone in this wing, so we have to answer it downstairs."

They ran to the nearest phone in the hall outside the living room. Diane answered it.

"Diane, it's Alec. We just learned from the highway patrol that the roads are being closed because of the snow. It looks like we'll have to stay the night in Lansing. I'm sorry to do this to you. Will you and Kathy be all right?"

Diane shivered. "I guess so. Are you sure you can't get home?"

"If we could, we would. We don't want to leave you and Kathy there alone. If you need anything, walk over to the Blacks' house. They'll help you. But don't go out tonight. Wait until morning, okay?"

"We'll be fine." But would they?

Slowly Diane hung up and turned to Kathy. "They can't get home because of the snow."

Kathy gulped. They were all alone in the big house. Then she smiled. They weren't alone! God was with them. "Let's turn off the lights upstairs and watch a video."

Trembling, Diane nodded. Maybe it wouldn't be so bad after all.

8

The Long Night

Diane clicked off the last bedroom light and breathed a sigh of relief. "Now we'll go watch a video. How about *Anne of Green Gables*?"

"And then *Anne of Avonlea*! It'll be eight hours of pure pleasure!" Kathy laughed. "We'll stay up all night and watch, then go to sleep. By the time we wake up, the roads should be open and your parents home."

Diane froze. "They aren't my parents. They're Alec and Nora."

"Oh, sorry." Kathy didn't know what to say, so she walked back downstairs silently.

In the den Diane pushed in the video, and they lay on the floor to watch, both wrapped in a blanket. Before twenty minutes passed they were sound asleep.

A noise buzzed around inside Kathy's head. Slowly she came out of her sleep and lifted her head. The video was still playing—Anne and Gil were talking. And the phone was ringing! Kathy shook Diane awake. "The phone."

Diane rubbed her eyes. "The phone? It can't be the phone."

"Then what's that sound?"

"It is the phone!" Diane awkwardly stood, then stumbled toward the phone in the hall. "Who'd call this late at night?"

Kathy followed her. "It's probably Nora and Alec checking up on us."

Diane answered the phone, then frowned. "It's for you."

Kathy took the phone. "Hello."

"I've been trying for three hours to get you!"

"Ty?" Kathy's head whirled. She was too tired to think clearly. "Why are you calling me?"

"I wanted to tell you about a movie I saw."

"Why?"

"I wanted to see what you were doing."

"I'm spending the night with Diane. It's really late, you know."

"It's snowing, and I'm bored."

Kathy yawned. "I'm sleepy."

"What took you so long to answer the phone?"

"We were asleep. I'm going to hang up." Kathy started to hang up. She could hear Ty shout "No!" until she dropped the receiver in place. She frowned and helplessly shook her head.

"He is really really weird." Diane shivered. "What's wrong with him anyway?"

Kathy shrugged. "He says he loves me."

"I sure wouldn't want him loving me if that's the way he acts."

Kathy walked slowly back to the den and sank to the edge of the couch while Diane sat in an armchair. On the TV Anne was talking to Marilla. Kathy couldn't hear what they said. All she heard was Diane saying over and over inside her head, "I sure wouldn't want him loving me if that's the way he acts."

"I'm hungry." Diane pushed herself up. "Want something to eat?"

Kathy yawned. "Not really, but I'll go with you."

Diane clicked off the VCR and the TV. The sudden silence filled the room.

As they walked into the kitchen, something struck the back door hard. The girls jumped and clung to each other.

"What was that?" Diane whispered.

"Maybe an animal lost in the snow," Kathy said in a low, tight voice. "Let's go see."

"No!" Diane held Kathy back. They stood side by side, staring at the door. "We don't dare open the door!"

"We have to help whatever or whoever it is."

Diane's eyes widened in alarm. "Do you think it could be a person?"

Trembling, Kathy nodded. "God is with us," she

said as much to herself as to Diane. "He'll take care of us."

Kathy pulled away from Diane and walked slowly to the back door. She clicked on the outside light and tried to see through the glass on the door. All she could see was swirling snow.

Diane peered out but couldn't see anything but snow either. "Maybe a tree fell against the door."

"It's not that windy out. Besides, your trees are way too big to get knocked down in this wind and snow."

"I guess you're right." Diane licked her dry lips with the tip of her tongue. "Are we going to open the door?"

"Yes." But Kathy didn't move. Her hands felt icy cold, and shivers ran up and down her spine. Maybe it would be wiser not to look. "It might be Tassel."

"It might be!"

Kathy took a deep breath and slowly opened the door. Cold air seeped around the still-closed storm door. Dare she open it? She pushed on the cold handle and pushed the door out. It went just so far and wouldn't go any further. "It's stuck."

Diane squeezed around Kathy and helped her push. It opened further, then stopped.

Kathy poked her head through the opening and gasped. A man lay in a crumpled heap, his arm and shoulder blocking the storm door. He wore a heavy coat but didn't have a hat on. Snowflakes partly covered his light brown hair. He moaned, and Kathy jumped.

Diane caught a glimpse of the man. She jumped back inside. "Leave him there, Kathy! He might be a killer!"

"Are you kidding? We can't leave him outdoors in the cold and snow!" Kathy pushed herself through the opening and pushed hard against the man to move him enough so she could open the door. He groaned, and her stomach lurched, but she pushed hard until finally she moved him. She opened the door wide and hooked it so it would stay open. "Help me, Diane."

"I can't!"

"Sure, you can. We'll have to drag him inside. He's too heavy to lift."

Diane hesitated, then slowly walked out to help Kathy. A blast of cold wind chilled her to the bone. They lifted the man's head and shoulders and tugged hard. He was limp but not dead. He groaned but didn't open his eyes. Finally they pulled him inside enough to close the doors, shutting out the icy wind and flying snow.

"Get blankets to cover him while I pull off his wet coat." Kathy tugged on the man's coat sleeve to try to get it off.

Diane hesitated, then raced for the stairs and the hall closet where the spare blankets were kept. She wouldn't let herself think about being upstairs alone.

She grabbed three blankets and a pillow, then raced back down, her feet loud on the steps.

Kathy eased the man up enough to take off his coat. He wore a sweater and jeans. His sneakers were soaking wet. She untied them and pulled them off. His thick gray socks were wet, and she pulled them off too. He had long toes and narrow feet.

Diane covered him with all three blankets while Kathy tucked the pillow under his head.

"He doesn't look hurt," Kathy whispered as she looked at the clean-shaven face.

"He's too clean and well-dressed to be a street person." Diane kept her voice low.

The man groaned, and his dark lashes fluttered. His face was ashen. He looked about the same age as Alec.

Kathy leaned close, but Diane leaped away.

"Help me," he whispered weakly.

"We could make him some tea," Diane suggested from a safe distance away.

"Yes! Do!" Kathy tucked the covers tighter around the man's bare feet. He was really cold. She could feel the chill rising from his body. "I wish we could get him on the couch and off the floor."

"He's too heavy." Diane looked toward the phone. "We could call Cal Black to help us."

Kathy nodded. "Maybe you should."

Diane hesitated, then walked to the phone. She picked it up and started to punch the number. She frowned, held the receiver away from her, and frowned again.

"What's wrong?" Kathy asked nervously.

"There's no dial tone."

Kathy leaped up and ran across the room. She snatched the phone from Diane and listened. It was indeed dead. Slowly, deliberately she hung up the receiver. "Now what?" she whispered.

Diane leaned heavily on the desk chair. "We can't go to the Blacks for help—not in the dark and the snow."

Kathy lifted her head high. "We'll be all right! We'll take care of this man! See if we don't!"

Diane slowly stood. Kathy looked and sounded so sure of herself. Maybe they *could* take care of the man. Maybe they weren't in trouble.

The man groaned and lifted his head a little.

Kathy dashed to his side and dropped down beside him. "We brought you inside. You'll be just fine."

Shivering, Diane stood back, her hands locked in front of her.

"Help . . . me . . . up." The man tried to sit but slumped back on the pillow.

Kathy slipped her arm under his head. "I'll help you. Try again."

He lifted his head, then his shoulders.

Diane rushed to his other side and helped the man sit up. She stood beside him, wondering if she should run away from him or stay there to keep him from falling back. She decided to follow Kathy's lead and stay put.

"Could you make it to a chair?" Kathy asked with a worried frown.

He looked toward the table and chairs. He pushed the blankets aside. "I can try."

Diane held onto him on one side and Kathy on the other. He stood, and they almost fell to their knees from his weight. He stumbled to a chair and dropped down on it. Kathy ran back for a blanket and draped it over him. Diane rushed to the stove and put on a pot of water.

"I'll make you tea." Diane's voice cracked, and she flushed.

"I'd prefer hot water with honey it in."

"Okay." Diane looked in the cupboard for the jar of honey.

Kathy sank to a chair next to the man. "Who are you, and what are you doing here?"

Diane held the honey jar and waited for the answer.

The man rubbed a hand over his light brown hair. "I'm Woods . . . Dan Woods. I was out in the storm and couldn't make it home."

"Where's your car?"

"Car?"

"Is it stuck in the snow?"

"Yes. Stuck in the snow."

The tea kettle whistled, and Diane quickly shut off the burner. She filled a cup with water and stirred in a spoonful of honey. Carefully she carried it to the table.

Dan Woods smiled. "Thanks."

Diane flushed. She sank to a chair on the other side of Kathy.

"Would you like something to eat?" Kathy asked. "We could make you something. A sandwich? Scrambled eggs?"

The man nodded. "I *am* hungry. Very hungry."

Kathy heated a can of chicken noodle soup while Diane fixed a grilled cheese sandwich. Diane filled a glass with apple juice and carried it to the table.

The smell of the sandwich made Kathy's stomach growl. She hadn't realized she was hungry. "I'm going to make myself a sandwich. Want one, Diane?"

"Sure. Thanks."

Soon the three sat at the table eating. The grandfather clock in the front hall bonged two o'clock.

"I feel much better." Dan Woods leaned back. The color had returned to his face. "I should be going." He stood, swayed, and sat back down. "But maybe not yet."

"We were watching *Anne of Green Gables*. Want to watch with us?" Diane wanted to bite out her tongue. She looked helplessly at Kathy.

Kathy smiled and nodded. "Yes, do! It's a great movie!"

Dan Woods smiled. "That's nice of you, but I don't think I could stay awake. But you girls go ahead. I'll rest here a bit longer, then leave."

The girls looked at each other and finally nodded. It would be too hard to sit there and try to think of something to say.

Kathy started to stand. She couldn't leave a stranger all alone in Diane's kitchen. "We'll stay with you until you go."

"Isn't your car stuck in the snow?" Diane asked.

"Yes. Stuck in the snow." He sighed heavily. "It's cold out there."

Diane wanted to offer him a bed in a spare room, but she didn't. It might not be safe.

Just then the back door opened.

Diane and Kathy leaped up, clung to each other, and stared at the door.

9

Sunday Surprises

Kathy gripped Diane's hand and watched the door swing wider. Who would just walk in at 2 in the morning?

Diane trembled and wanted to hide, but Kathy held her to the spot. Cold air rushed in along with a few snowflakes that melted immediately.

Alec and Nora stepped into sight and stamped snow off their boots. They looked cold and tired.

Kathy let out her breath. Diane almost collapsed in relief.

"We made it," Nora said.

"We got behind a snow plow." Alec's voice faded away as he looked past the girls at Dan Woods. Alec's brows shot up. "Who are you, and what are you doing here?" Before Dan could answer, Alec turned on the girls. "Why in the world did you let a stranger into the house? Do you know how dangerous that is?"

Diane backed away from Alec's anger. She'd seen him angry before, but never at her.

Kathy cleared her throat. "He fell outside the door and was unconscious. We couldn't leave him to freeze out there."

"Of course you couldn't!" Nora patted Kathy's arm and pulled Diane to her side. "Let's give them a chance to tell us the story."

Dan Woods stood unsteadily to his feet. "I'll get out of your way." He swayed and dropped back to the chair. "I guess I won't. I'm Dan Woods, and I didn't mean any harm. Your girls were nice enough to help me. I thought I might die in the snow."

Diane looked beseechingly at Nora. "We have lots of empty beds. Can't he sleep in one of them?"

"His car is stuck in the snow," Kathy added. "We dragged him in and got him warm and fed him. We can't just toss him back out."

Nora looked at Alec. "Well?"

Alec sighed. "All right . . . All right . . . I won't kick him out." He took Nora's coat and hung hers and his in the closet, then sat at the table. "I didn't see your car out there."

"It's probably on the other side of the hill," Diane said. "Don't ask him too many questions. He's not feeling well."

Dan smiled at Diane and Kathy. "I'm much better now. I'll get out of here in a few minutes. And I'll be all right."

"You're staying the night," Nora said firmly. "That's settled."

Alec crossed his arms over his chest. "We can't have you collapsing in our yard."

"Then I'll stay the night, but I'll get out of your way when I wake up." Dan rubbed an unsteady hand over his face.

Alec jumped up. "I'll help you upstairs so you can go to bed now."

"Thank you." Dan stood, weaving unsteadily.

Alec gripped Dan's arm and slowly, carefully walked him upstairs.

Nora studied the girls thoughtfully. "What else happened tonight that you're not telling?"

Diane shrugged. "The electricity went out for over two hours."

"That's terrible! Did you get cold?"

"A little."

Kathy could've told about Ty calling, but she didn't. They didn't know Ty, so why bother? "We saw the horses and talked to Stuart and Elaine Black."

"That's nice." Nora yawned. "Excuse me. You girls go on up to bed. The roads are too bad for us to go to church in the morning, so sleep in as late as you want."

The girls said good night and walked slowly to Diane's room. Within minutes they fell asleep and slept until almost noon. As Kathy dressed she smelled toast and coffee. Her stomach cramped with hunger.

Sunlight streamed through the windows. She looked out at a snow-covered countryside. The snow glistened like a million diamonds.

Diane stepped from the closet where she'd dressed in jeans and a long pink sweater. "I'm hungry!"

"Me too." Kathy pushed her sweater sleeves up to her elbows and hurried downstairs with Diane. "I wonder if Dan Woods is still here."

"I hope he's feeling better. It was fun helping him." Diane walked into the kitchen, where Alec and Nora were having coffee.

"Morning," they said.

"Hi." Diane glanced quickly around. "Is Dan Woods still in bed?"

Kathy saw the quick look pass between Alec and Nora. Something was up.

"He was gone when we got up," Nora said, keeping her voice light.

Alec scowled. "I checked to see if anything was missing, but so far nothing is."

"He didn't seem like a thief." Diane lifted her chin defiantly. Didn't they trust her at all? "Besides, he was too weak to sneak through the house and steal things!"

"I hope he isn't lying out in the snow somewhere." Kathy peered out the window and strained to see all around the yard. "I don't even see any footprints."

Alec jumped up and looked out. "The wind probably swept them away already."

A chill slithered down Diane's back. Maybe Dan Woods just wanted them to think he left. Maybe he was hiding in the house somewhere, waiting for the right opportunity. Diane frowned. She didn't trust her own judgment any more than Alec did! With a sigh she pulled a box of raisin bran out of the cupboard and poured a bowlful. "Want some cereal, Kathy?"

"Sure." Kathy fixed a bowl of raisin bran and carried it to the table. At home she always added extra raisins from the bag Mom kept in the refrigerator for snacks. "It feels funny not going to church."

Nora nodded. "I know." She waited until Diane and Alec sat down. "When I was a kid the thing I really liked about Sunday was coming home after church to a houseful of the most delicious aromas—roast beef or turkey cooking in the oven. Mom always fixed dinner so it would bake in the oven while we were gone. It seemed to smell better on Sunday than on any other day."

Diane leaned back in her chair. "In South America we had a housekeeper to cook for us. She couldn't get used to making food we liked." Diane stopped short. She hadn't thought about anything concerning her parents except their terrible death while she played with Elisa for a long, long time. Her throat closed over, and she couldn't finish the story.

Kathy felt the sudden tension. Her chewing sounded loud in the silence, so she stopped. The flakes grew mushy in her mouth.

Nora chuckled. "I think I'd like a housekeeper." The tension was broken, and they talked about the pros and cons of having a housekeeper.

Kathy finished her cereal. When they were alone she'd ask Diane what had caused the tension.

Several minutes later Kathy and Diane bundled up to go outdoors. Kathy's skin pricked with heat while she waited for Diane to find her other mitten.

Alec smiled at Kathy as he stood by the door with his hands in the pockets of his jeans. "I told your dad I'd take you home as soon as the snow plow goes through. So if you're outdoors and see it, come in and tell me."

"I will." Kathy wanted to get home to call the Best Friends and tell them all that had happened.

"I'm ready." Diane's cheeks were red with heat.

Alec opened the door. "Have fun building a snowman, girls."

"We will." Kathy thankfully stepped outdoors. The cold air felt great. The sun was so bright, she had to squint to see.

"I never built a snowman before." Diane picked up a handful of snow and packed it into a ball. She threw it at a tree, but it sailed past and hit the ground.

Just then they heard a shout near the barn. Stuart and Elaine were climbing the fence and calling to them. They were both dressed in bright blue snowpants and jackets.

"Let's see if they'll help us," Kathy said as she ran to meet them.

Diane hesitated, then followed at a slower pace. Would they make fun of her because she didn't know how to build a snowman?

When they all stood together Stuart looked questioningly at Diane. "Who was the man I saw leaving your house early this morning?"

Diane's heart leaped. He *had* left! He wasn't hiding inside! "Dan Woods. Why?"

"We saw him near the barn a few days ago and wondered who he was." Elaine's eyes sparkled. "We called to him, but he hurried away like he didn't hear us."

Diane's stomach lurched. "Where'd he go?"

Stuart pointed to the woods at the far side of the house. "Back there. He went there again this morning."

Kathy bit her lip. Was there a mystery surrounding Dan Woods? If only Hannah were here to solve it!

"What about his car?" Diane asked sharply.

Elaine shrugged. "We didn't see a car. He was walking."

"He said he got stuck last night." Kathy looked up and down the road. There wasn't a car in sight. "Let's look on the other side of the hill and see if it's there."

"It's not," Stuart said. "We can see the other side of the hill from our upstairs window."

Diane's skin pricked with fear. "Why would he lie to us?"

"He really was unconscious, and he really was weak." Kathy kicked at a clump of snow. "Maybe he didn't have a car. Maybe he said so because we said so."

Stuart looked toward the woods. "Let's see if we can find him . . . Or maybe his trail." He headed toward the woods with Elaine close on his heels.

Elaine glanced over her shoulder at Kathy and Diane. "Are you coming?"

They looked at each other, shrugged, and ran after Stuart and Elaine.

In the woods Kathy walked between two giant snow-covered pines. A blue jay scolded and flew away. It was warmer among the trees than in the open yard. She pulled off her mittens and stuffed them into her pockets. The cool air against her hot hands felt refreshing.

Diane leaned against a tree and studied the ground around her. "Do you see anything, Stuart?" she called.

"Not yet!" He was out of sight, and his voice drifted back to them.

Suddenly a snowball splatted against Diane's leg. She squealed and jumped.

"Got ya!" Laughing, Elaine peeked around a tree at the edge of the woods. "Me and Kathy against Stuart and Diane!"

Diane ducked around a tree. She'd never in her life had a snowball fight. She scooped up snow and pressed it into a ball. She peeked out just as a snowball flew toward her. She ducked back, and it sailed past. She looked out, took aim, and threw her ball at Kathy. It struck her in the shoulder. Diane giggled and jumped back behind the tree.

With a shout Kathy leaped from behind her tree and pitched three snowballs in a row at Diane. One grazed her on the arm, and the rest missed badly. While Kathy was in sight, Stuart hit her with two snowballs. She laughed as she scooped up more snow. She hit something hard. She thought it was a stick but looked closer. It was a house key! She brushed it off and shouted, "Hey, look what I found!" She stepped into sight and was struck again. "Wait! Look!"

Diane's stomach knotted, and for a minute she couldn't move. Finally she walked over to Kathy. Stuart and Elaine were already looking at what Kathy held. Diane shivered. "What is it?"

"A key."

"It looks like our house key," Diane whispered.

"Did your parents or you lose it?" Kathy wanted to grab back the word *parents*, but it was too late.

Diane shook her head. "I have my key in my purse in my room. Alec and Nora would've said something if they'd lost a key."

"Let's see what door it fits." Stuart reached for the key, but Diane snatched it out of Kathy's hand.

Diane scowled at Stuart. "*I'll* see what it fits!"

Stuart shrugged. "Okay."

Diane ran to the house with the others beside her. She tried the back door first. The key fit. "It's for the back door! I didn't think it would be."

"Could I look at it closer?" Stuart held out his hand.

Diane hesitated, then laid it in his hand.

"What?" Elaine asked.

Kathy could see by Stuart's face that he had discovered something important.

"It's not rusted at all. It's not even dirty. Whoever dropped it did it since it rained last or it would have dirt in the grooves."

"I'll ask Nora and Alec." Diane took the key. "Wait here. I'll be right back." Inside, heat rushed at her. She pulled off her cap. Her hair crackled and stood on end from static electricity. "Nora? Alec? Where are you?"

"In my study," Nora called.

Diane pulled off her boots and ran to the study. She held out the key and told them where Kathy had found it. They both checked, and each had their own key. "Maybe whoever was coming in and out of the house used this key."

Alec impatiently shook his head. "You don't give up, do you?"

Nora sighed. "Just supposing that's true—and I'm not saying it is!—but suppose it's true—now whoever had the key won't have a way in. So now we have nothing to be concerned about."

"Maybe it's *your* key." Alec tapped Diane on the nose. "Did you check to see?"

She flushed. "I didn't check, but I know my key's in my purse."

"Run upstairs and see." Nora smiled. "It's better to know for sure."

Diane closed her hand over the key and ran to the stairs and on up. She knew her key was safely in her purse. She carried it to school all the time just in case neither Nora nor Alec were home when she got off the bus.

In her room she opened the drawer where she kept her purse and looked inside. Just wait until she showed them two keys!

"Where is that key?" she muttered as she rummaged around. She finally dumped the contents of her purse onto her desk and pushed aside the stick of gum, a pack of tissues, a pencil, a small notepad, a folded English assignment paper.

She shivered and sank weakly to the chair. Her key was not there! She looked at the key they'd found. There was something different about it from hers. What was it? She studied it a little longer. Suddenly it hit her. It was gold. Hers was silver.

"Someone took my key," she whispered hoarsely. "But who?"

10

The Lie

Her stomach fluttering, Diane held her head high as she faced Alec and Nora. "My key is right where I said it was—in my purse." The lie burned her tongue, but she wouldn't take it back. "This key isn't mine." That wasn't a lie. If she'd said it wasn't her key, and that hers was missing, they'd just think she couldn't remember how her own key looked.

"Probably the Bellwoods had a spare key and somehow lost it in the woods." Alec shrugged. "Don't make a mystery out of it, Diane."

"I won't." But she knew it was indeed a mystery. And when Kathy heard, she'd think so too. "I'm going back out now." She dropped the key in the front pocket of her jeans. "Stuart and Elaine are here, and we're having a snowball fight."

"Sounds like fun." Nora sighed as she leaned back and locked her hands behind her head. Her computer hummed. "I remember the snowball fights

99

I used to have with Kathy's mom. We had a lot of fun."

Diane hurried away before Nora got started on another story about her childhood. The stories were fun to listen to, but sometimes they were too long.

Outdoors Diane told the others about her missing key. "I don't know what happened to it."

"Maybe it fell out at school," Stuart said.

"Maybe." But Diane didn't believe it.

"If it did, somebody will turn it in at the office." Elaine nodded solemnly.

Just then a bell rang. The clear tones drifted out over the countryside.

Elaine looked toward her home. "That's Mom calling us home."

Stuart scowled. "What a rotten time to have to leave. Let us know what you learn, will you?"

Diane nodded.

Elaine twisted her hands nervously. "Don't go looking in the woods for that man all by yourselves, though. Something awful could happen."

Diane shivered.

Kathy bit her lip.

"We'll try to come again later this afternoon." Stuart lifted his hand in a wave and ran to the driveway with Elaine at his heels. They crossed the road and ran to their own driveway. Barking, Tassel ran to meet them.

Pulling on her mittens, Diane turned to Kathy. "Shall we look for Dan Woods?"

"Alone? Just the two of us?"

Diane nodded.

"I don't know. Maybe your dad would go with us."

Diane jabbed Kathy's arm. "He is *not* my dad! I told you that."

"Sorry." Kathy narrowed her eyes. "But . . . since they adopted you, they really are your mom and dad."

"I don't think of them that way. I only want one daddy and one mommy." Tears stung Diane's eyes, but she blinked them away. She'd already cried all she was going to in front of Kathy.

"You're going to miss out on a lot, Diane." Kathy traced a line in the snow with the toe of her boot. Finally she looked at Diane. "It's good to have a mom and dad to talk to, to listen to, and just to be quiet with."

Diane tossed her head. "I can do that with Alec and Nora."

"Not if you don't let them get close enough to love you. And not if you don't let yourself love them." Kathy took a step closer to Diane. "Why don't you want to love them?"

Diane rubbed her nose with the back of her hand. Her mitten was soggy against her face. "I can't love them, Kathy. Don't you understand? I don't deserve to, and I don't deserve to have them love me."

"Why not?"

"I told you why," Diane whispered around the lump in her throat. Abruptly she turned away. "Oh, forget it! I don't want to think about it or talk about it! Let's solve the mystery of this key. And let's look for Dan Woods."

A snowmobile with two people on it roared along the side of the road and stopped at the end of the drive. The girls turned to watch. Someone dressed in a black and silver snowmobile suit jumped off and ran up the driveway. The driver leaned forward as the snowmobile roared off, disappearing out of sight on the other side of the hill. Finally the sound faded and was gone.

Diane and Kathy watched the person run across the yard. It was impossible to tell if it was a boy or girl or a small man or woman. The person waved.

"Kathy!"

She gasped. She knew that voice. He pulled off his cap, and she saw the blond hair. It was Ty Wilton! Her knees grew weak. She didn't know if she was happy or angry. She couldn't find her voice to speak to him.

"Who is it?" Diane asked sharply.

"Ty," Kathy whispered.

Ty stopped in front of Kathy and smiled at her as if he were the happiest person in the world. "I heard you got snowed in, so I came to see you."

"You shouldn't have," Kathy said weakly. She turned to Diane. "Diane, this is Ty Wilton."

"Get out of here," Diane snapped. "You're trespassing."

Ty scowled at her. "What's wrong with you? I came to see Kathy."

"She doesn't want you here!"

Ty chuckled. "She and I are going together."

"What?" Kathy cried.

Ty smiled at Kathy. "We're going together."

Kathy jumped back. "We are not!"

"You're only saying that because Diane is listening."

"I'm saying it because it's true!" Anger rushed through Kathy. "You can't stay here, Ty. Go home."

"How can I? It's a long way to walk."

Diane rolled her eyes. "You're a total jerk! How did you expect to get back?"

"With Kathy."

"But I can't go until the snow plow goes through. What if it doesn't come until tomorrow?"

Chuckling, Ty shrugged. "I didn't think about that."

"It's about time you did think!"

Diane glanced back toward the woods. Her breath caught in her throat. Was she seeing right? She closed her eyes and opened them again. Dan Woods was leaning against a pine tree, his head down. He wore his coat but no hat. Diane grabbed Kathy and yanked her around. "Look! It's Dan Woods!"

Kathy started toward him. "Let's talk to him."

Ty caught her arm. "Where are you going? I came to see you."

"We're going to talk to that man." Kathy pulled away from Ty and ran beside Diane toward Dan.

"I'm coming too," Ty called as he ran after them.

Kathy dashed around Diane and reached Dan Woods first. He looked terrible. "Hi. Are you feeling sick again?"

"I'm burning up," he whispered.

"Did you get your car out?" Diane asked sharply.

Dan moaned, and his knees buckled. He clung to the tree to keep from falling.

"You're still sick!" Kathy wrung her hands and tried to figure out how to help him.

"Why didn't you stay in bed longer?" Diane stood helplessly beside him. She turned to Ty. "Don't just stand there! Help him to the house!"

"Sure . . . Okay." Ty put his arm around Dan's waist. Ty was a few inches shorter than Dan. "Hold on to me and I'll walk you to the house."

"I can't get back in. Lost my key," Dan muttered.

The girls looked at each other and mouthed, "Key?"

"Where's your house?" Kathy asked.

Diane held her breath.

Dan stumbled, and Ty almost fell to his knees.

"We better get him inside." Ty staggered, then struggled to stand. "Help me!"

Diane stepped to Dan's other side, and together she and Ty walked Dan to the back door.

Kathy opened the door and held it wide. The smell of popcorn drifted out. She saw the flush on Dan's face like he had a fever. Maybe he had the flu, or something worse.

Diane eased Dan to a kitchen chair, then turned and called, "Nora! Alec! Come here quick!"

They rushed in and stopped short when they saw Dan.

"What's he doing back?" Alec snapped.

"He's sick!" Nora touched her hand to Dan's face. "He's burning up!" She turned to Alec. "Get him upstairs. See that he takes a shower, then give him a pair of your flannel pajamas to wear. I'll fix him some soup."

Diane's eye widened. Nora was actually going to take care of Dan Woods, and he was a stranger to her! And Alec was going to let Dan wear his pajamas even though he didn't trust the man! Tears of gratitude filled Diane's eyes. Pride in Nora and Alec rose in her.

Later Diane and Kathy walked back outdoors with Ty. Nora had asked them to be quiet so Dan could rest. The warm sun had melted some of the snow.

Ty scooped up a handful of snow, pressed it into a ball, and pitched it at a tree. It splatted against the trunk, leaving a splotch of snow. Frowning thoughtfully, he turned to the girls. "I've seen that man before, but I can't remember where."

"He must live around here since he's walking instead of driving." Diane looked up at the bedroom window where she knew Dan was resting. "We'll have to let his family know he's here."

"He's too well dressed to be a street person," Ty said.

Kathy nodded. "That's what Diane said last night. But I don't know if he lives around here. Stuart and Elaine didn't know him."

"He said he dropped his key." Diane's voice broke, and she shivered. "We found a key. Do you think . . ." Her voice trailed off.

Kathy kicked a clump of snow. A horse whinnied. Across the road Tassel barked. "It can't be what we're thinking. How would he get a key to your house, and why would he call your house his house?"

Ty slapped his glove against his arm. "I've got it! The man looks like Grandpa's picture of Seth Bellwood! The one with my Uncle Dan."

Kathy frowned at Ty. He'd do anything to impress her. "Don't make up a story just to sound important."

"What do you mean?"

Kathy shook her finger at him. "You know what I mean. It won't do any good to make up stories. He doesn't really look like Seth Bellwood, does he?"

Ty looked hurt. "He does too!"

"Maybe he's Aaron . . . But he can't be Aaron Bellwood," Diane snapped. "He's dead."

A chill ran down Kathy's spine. She pushed her hands into her jacket pockets. "What if Aaron Bellwood really isn't dead? What if Dan Woods *is* Aaron Bellwood?"

Diane gasped. Was it possible?

"We could ask my grandpa," Ty said excitedly. "He'd know."

Diane's eyes sparkled. "We'll have to keep Dan Woods here until your grandpa can see him." Diane laughed breathlessly. "Aaron Bellwood could have a key to the house, right?"

Kathy nodded. Her legs felt weak at the thought of the runaway boy coming back home when he was a man only to find his parents gone. "Ty, does your grandpa know where the Bellwoods live now?"

"I don't know, but I'll ask. Want me to call him right now?"

Kathy turned to Diane. "What do you think?"

Diane narrowed her eyes in thought. In the distance a snowmobile roared. "Ask him, but don't tell him why. It would be really embarrassing if Dan Woods is who he says he is and not Aaron Bellwood."

"You're right," Kathy said.

"I'll call now." Ty hurried toward the back door. Before he could open it, he heard a snowmobile stopping at the end of the driveway.

"Need a ride, Ty?" the man shouted.

Ty hesitated. "Be right there!" He grinned sheepishly. "I guess I better get back to Middle Lake. I'll call my grandpa when I get home."

"Thanks, Ty." Diane smiled. "Call me when you know."

He nodded and ran across the yard. He looked over his shoulder and shouted, "See ya, Kathy!"

She lifted her hand and barely waved.

"He's not as bad as I thought he'd be," Diane said softly.

"I know." Kathy sighed. "But he's not a Christian. He doesn't even go to church."

"Oh." Diane watched until the snowmobile was out of sight. "We need to pray for him." She laughed right out loud. "I haven't thought about praying for someone else for a long time. Kathy, you and the Best Friends are a good influence."

Kathy smiled. "Thanks."

Just then Alec stuck his head out the back door. He looked upset. "Diane, come here! You too, Kathy. I have something you both should see."

They glanced at each other and shivered.

11

The Key

With her icy hands locked in her lap, Diane sat in Nora's study with Kathy on the couch beside her. Nora sat at her desk, her computer off, her face stern. She'd chewed the lipstick off her bottom lip. His face red, Alec paced the floor. His stocking feet were silent on the carpet. From time to time he jangled the change in his pockets.

Kathy glanced toward the window. How she wished she was home. Or with the Best Friends. Why was Alec so angry? Was he going to explode? Kathy bit back a whimper. How she hated to be yelled at! And just as bad, she hated to be present when someone else was being yelled at.

Diane looked down at her icy hands in her lap and waited. Alec was really mad at her. Would he send her off to a foster home and tear up the adoption papers? Her heart jerked. She didn't want to go back to foster homes. She wanted . . . parents! The realization almost took her breath away. When had she started wanting parents and not just a permanent home? Had it happened because of her talk with Kathy about God's great love?

Alec grabbed a key off Nora's desk and held it almost under Diane's nose. "Look at this, Diane!"

She shrank down into herself. It was her key, the key missing from her purse. It was silver, and it had the tiny spot of red fingernail polish Nora had painted on it so they'd know it was her key to the back door if they found it around the house. In the excitement she had forgotten about the fingernail polish until now, and they must've too or they would've known the key Kathy had found under the tree wasn't hers. She trembled so badly, she thought she'd fall off the couch.

"Where did you find it?" Kathy asked in a tiny voice.

"It fell out of Dan Woods's pocket when he undressed. He didn't notice, but I did." Alec held the key right up to Diane's face. "Why did you give that stranger the key to our back door?"

Diane leaped up. Dan Woods had stolen the key from her purse! She knew that beyond a shadow of a doubt. "I didn't give it to him!"

"Then how did he get it?"

"From my purse."

"When would he? You told us about an hour ago the key was in your purse."

Diane's words died in her throat. She had said that very thing!

Nora brushed tears from her eyes. "You've lied to us over and over. We can't take it anymore."

Diane stared in horror at Nora and Alec. They had known about her lies all along and hadn't said anything!

Alec knotted his fists at his sides. "Telling us your key was in your purse when it wasn't, and now telling us you didn't give it to Dan Woods, is too much! We thought we could teach you to trust us, but we can't. You're determined to keep us at arm's length. You're determined to continue lying. How can we help you if you don't want help?"

Her cheeks fiery red, Diane shook her head. "I did not give Dan Woods my key! Honest! He must've stolen it from my purse."

Nora threw up her hands. "That's it! Go to your room, Diane. We'll talk to you later when we're calmer."

Alec turned his back on them and stared out the window.

Nora suddenly realized Kathy was there. It was too bad she'd witnessed the terrible scene. She sighed. "Kathy, go on up with Diane. As soon as we can, we'll take you home."

Kathy nodded. She was trembling so badly she didn't know if she could walk. She hated hearing the Brewsters yell at Diane.

Her head down, Diane walked out of the study.

A few minutes later Diane sank to her desk chair and looked at Kathy as she collapsed in a chair at the small table. The room was too warm from the sun shining in the windows. A hint of strawberry shampoo hung in the air from the connecting bathroom. "I didn't give Dan Woods my key," Diane whispered. She was afraid if she spoke aloud she'd burst into tears.

"I know." Kathy touched a yellow chrysanthemum. "But when would he have taken it?"

"I don't know! It was in there when I got home from school Friday."

"You didn't have your purse with you Saturday."

"How would he even know to look in my purse?" Diane shivered.

Kathy gasped. "Yes! How would he?"

"And why would he want it? Does he plan to rob us when we're gone?"

Kathy jumped up. "Let's go talk to him."

"I don't know . . ." Diane licked her dry lips. "What if he hurts us?"

"He's weak from being sick, so what can he do to two strong girls?" Kathy tugged Diane to her feet. "Let's go before I have to leave." She wanted to know how it was going to turn out.

They ran down the hall, across the connecting living room, and into the other hall. At the sound of voices, they ducked into an empty bedroom. Kathy left the door ajar, so they could hear and see what was going on.

"It's Alec and Nora," Diane whispered. "They're probably checking on Dan Woods."

Kathy saw the Brewsters walk out of the bedroom across the hall and one door up. They looked upset as they walked.

"I'm calling the police," Alec said in a low, tight voice as he walked past where Kathy and Diane were hiding. "I want that man jailed!"

"He doesn't seem like a criminal, but we can't take chances," Nora said. "He doesn't have any identification on him. I don't think his name is Dan Woods."

Kathy and Diane stared in shock at each other. Why would they have the police arrest Dan Woods? He hadn't done anything wrong. But maybe he planned to.

"We have to talk to him," Diane whispered.

Kathy inched open the door, waited another minute, then crept out with Diane on her heels. They hurried down the hall and slipped inside Dan's room. He was asleep, his arms flung across the bed and his hair damp.

Diane looked down at the sleeping man. He looked younger and very vulnerable. "I hate to wake him up."

"I know." Kathy touched Dan's shoulder. His

pajamas felt soft and warm. "But we have to." She shook him a little, then shook him harder.

He moaned.

Diane and Kathy jumped back, then giggled. Kathy stepped back up to the bed and shook Dan again.

He opened his eyes, then smiled. "Hello, girls. Thanks for helping me." His eyes drooped as if he were going right back to sleep.

"Stay awake!" Diane locked her hands under her chin. "We have to talk to you."

"What about?"

A shiver trickled down Kathy's spine. Was it wise to talk to Dan Woods? Maybe they should let the police take him in for questioning.

"Why'd you take my key?" Diane blurted out.

"I lost mine."

Diane pulled the key from her pocket "Is this it?"

He took it and nodded.

"But it's to our back door!"

Kathy moved nervously from one foot to the other. "Why do you have a key to this house?"

Diane frowned. "How'd you even know to look in my purse for a key?"

Dan eased himself up until he was half sitting. "I've been in and out of the house for a month now. I watched you unlock the back door with your key, then drop it in your purse. I knew which room was yours. I sneaked in one night and took your key while you all were sleeping." He sank back down. "I didn't take your key to do anything wrong or to get you in trouble. I lost mine, and I had to get back inside."

"Lost *yours?*" Kathy cried.

Diane stepped back from the bed, her heart hammering. Was something wrong with the man? He talked about coming in and out of the house as if it were his! Could it be . . . ?

Dan picked up the glass of water Alec had left on the nightstand for him and drank thirstily. He set the glass down and sank weakly to his pillow. "My head is a little fuzzy."

Diane finally found her voice and asked, "Why did you come in our house?"

Dan frowned. "It's *my* house."

"No! We bought it!"

"When?"

"Last month."

Dan groaned. "Does that mean they're never coming back?"

"Who?"

"Seth and Lindy Bellwood."

Diane shot a look of astonishment at Kathy, then turned back to Dan. "What do you know about them?"

Kathy leaned down toward Dan. She could smell his fever. "Who *are* you?"

He sighed heavily. "I suppose I'd better tell you the truth . . . I am Aaron Bellwood."

The girls gasped and stared at him in astonishment, then at each other.

Dan Woods, who was really Aaron Bellwood, rubbed an unsteady hand over his eyes. "Seth and Lindy Bellwood are my parents. They own this estate."

Kathy couldn't believe her ears.

Diane shook her head. "Nora and Alec Brewster own it. They bought it over a month ago."

His face ashen and his eyes wide in alarm, Aaron Bellwood pushed himself up. "Where are my folks?"

"We don't know. They moved about five years ago."

Kathy moved restlessly. "Somebody said you died."

He frowned. "Died? You can see I'm alive."

Kathy tried to think of something to say. What would Hannah say at a time like this? Suddenly Kathy knew. "How do we know you're telling the truth?"

"My wallet is in the back of the nightstand in the room across the hall. That's the room I've been sleeping in."

Diane clamped her hand over her mouth. It was the very room where she'd found the dead leaf under the bed and the open window. It was the room she'd heard noises in at different times.

"We'll go look." Kathy tugged on Diane's arm. They had to stay together just in case the man was dangerous.

In the hall Diane whispered hoarsely, "Do you believe him?"

"I don't know." Kathy's legs felt like Jello left out of the refrigerator too long.

In the bedroom Diane opened the nightstand drawer and reached to the back. She touched something and jumped back with a tiny squeal. "There is something in there!"

Kathy peeked into the drawer. "It is a wallet." She gingerly pulled out the trifold black leather wallet and opened it. "Here's his driver's license."

"He *is* Aaron Bellwood!" Diane sank weakly down on the bed. He looked healthier in the picture, but it was indeed the same man. "And I don't think he's here to steal anything."

Kathy nodded in agreement. "I think he's here to find his parents."

Diane shot up. "And Alec and Nora are calling the police! We've got to stop them!"

"Unless it's already too late."

"Let's go!" Diane raced for the stairs.

Kathy clutched the wallet to her and ran after Diane. Their stocking feet were quiet on the hall floor and on the steps.

"Nora! Alec!" Diane shouted. She couldn't take the time to search the house until she found them.

"In my study," Nora answered.

Diane dashed to the study. Her chest rose and

fell. Her cheeks were red, and her eyes flashed with excitement. "Did you call the police?"

Nora nodded.

Alec frowned as he jumped up from the couch, his guitar in his hand. "How'd you know we were going to call them?"

"Look!" Kathy thrust the wallet at Alec before the fighting began.

Nora darted around her desk and looked at the wallet with Alec.

As quickly as she could, Diane told them what Aaron Bellwood had said. Kathy spoke up a few times.

"So, call the police back and tell them not to come." Diane took a deep breath and expectantly looked at Nora and Alec. "Please. Please?"

They looked at each other a long time, then at Diane.

Diane twisted her hands, and her stomach cramped. Were they going to do what she asked, or were they too upset with her?

Kathy leaned weakly against the desk and silently prayed for them to do the right thing.

Alec strode to the desk and snatched up the phone. "I'll tell them we made a mistake."

Diane's eyes filled with tears. She squeezed Alec's arm. "Thanks."

He smiled at her.

Just then someone knocked on the back door.

"Oh, no!" Diane pressed her hand to her heart. "It's too late!"

Kathy thought about Aaron Bellwood upstairs in bed, not knowing the police were coming to get him. She wanted to run up the stairs and warn him, but she couldn't make herself move.

"I'll get the door." Nora hurried out of her study.

Kathy hesitated, then ran after her.

"Sorry, Diane." Alec hung up, slipped an arm around Diane's shoulders, and walked after the others.

Diane jerked away from Alec. "I have to tell Aaron Bellwood what's going on!"

Alec caught her hand. "No! Wait!"

Glaring, Diane jerked away and ran for the stairs.

12

Best Friends

Chelsea stopped right in the middle of stirring the chocolate-chip cookies she was making with Roxie and Hannah. They stood across the island counter from her. Both had just taken a fingerful of dough. "I think Kathy's in trouble."

Roxie gasped.

Hannah popped the dough into her mouth and chewed it. It was sweet and the chips hard and bitter-sweet. She nodded and swallowed. "Let's pray for her."

Roxie swallowed the bite in her mouth and frowned. "How do you know something's wrong with Kathy?"

Chelsea smiled. "I can tell in my heart. The Holy Spirit is letting me know."

"Is that true?" Roxie looked at Hannah for confirmation.

Hannah nodded.

The girls held hands over the island counter and prayed for Kathy, then for Diane and the Brewsters.

When they finished, Chelsea started stirring the dough again. "I'm going to call the Abers and see if they're going to pick up Kathy. Maybe we can go along."

"Good idea." Hannah nodded as she took over from Chelsea. Hannah sprinkled a little more flour in the dough. None of them liked thin cookies. But they didn't like them too thick either. They'd learned to judge when they had added the right amount of flour by the feel of the dough.

"I wonder if the road has been cleared yet." Roxie looked out the window. The sun had melted a lot of the snow, but she'd heard it had snowed harder out where the Brewsters lived.

Chelsea impatiently tapped her toe as she listened to the Abers' phone ring for the fourth time. She was ready to hang up when Grace Aber answered. Chelsea asked about Kathy.

Grace laughed. "It's funny you should ask. I'm getting ready to go after her right now. I tried calling, but the line was busy, so I'll just surprise them. I borrowed a four-wheel drive van just in case the road isn't plowed. Would you like to go with me?"

"Yes! Hannah and Roxie too?"

"Certainly. I'll be there in a couple of minutes."

"We'll be ready." Chelsea hung up and laughed. "She'll be here to get us in a few minutes!"

Hannah scraped off the stirring spoon. "We'll put the dough in the refrigerator and finish when we get back."

"We'll call our folks and let them know we're going." Roxie reached for the phone.

"And I'll run upstairs and tell Mom. She's playing a computer game with Rob." Chelsea dashed down the hall to the stairs.

Several minutes later the Best Friends rode with Grace Aber out into the country. Grace wore sunglasses to ward off the glare of the sun on the snow. The road was slushy but safe. Partly melted snowmen stood in the front yards of many of the farms they passed.

Chelsea watched a dog race along the edge of the road. It was barking, but she couldn't hear it over the hum of the van's heater. What was Kathy doing right now? Chelsea smiled. It seemed like an entire month instead of a day since she'd seen Kathy.

Roxie kept her eyes glued to the road. She wanted to see the horses Diane had said they boarded at their place. Roxie unzipped her jacket. She'd be glad to see Kathy too, of course, but it had been only yesterday since they'd been together at Mr. Parker's. He had paid them more than he'd agreed on when they finished cleaning the basement. "You girls worked hard and did a first-rate job," he'd said as he handed a check to Chelsea to cash and distribute among them. "I'll have you come over regularly so it never gets that bad again." Because of that, they'd agreed. Otherwise, they had decided to never work for him again. So far they'd only had three people in their book they'd never do jobs for again.

Hannah pushed her long, shiny hair back and silently prayed for Kathy and Diane. It was going to be fun to see the Bellwood Estate. Maybe Diane would take them through it and tell them more about the mystery. Maybe they could even help solve the mystery!

Grace Aber finally pulled into the slushy driveway and up to the four-car garage. "Here we are, girls."

They sat in silence, taking in every detail of the place.

"We'll use the back door." Grace slipped out of the warm car. Chilly wind blew against her, fluttering her short brown hair. She pushed her sunglasses onto the top of her head. "Coming, girls?"

They scrambled out of the car and ran to the back door, their boots leaving big holes in the soft snow. Chelsea knocked.

"I'll finally get to go inside this house," Hannah whispered, shivering with excitement.

"It's beautiful inside." Grace reached around Chelsea and knocked again. "It's as beautiful inside as out. The rooms are huge!"

The Best Friends looked at each other and grinned.

Inside the house Diane raced up the stairs, taking them two at a time. She couldn't let anything happen to Aaron Bellwood! She and Kathy had practically saved his life. They were responsible for him. She wasn't going to let the police take him in for questioning.

She burst into the bedroom. The bed was empty! Aaron Bellwood was gone!

Downstairs Kathy stood behind Nora Brewster as she opened the back door. Kathy held her breath, expecting to see the police. Instead she saw her mom and the Best Friends!

"Grace!" Nora cried, pulling her into the hall.

"We came for Kathy," Grace said as she stepped aside and made room for the girls to rush in.

Kathy hugged her mom, then turned to the girls. Her eyes shone. "You don't know how glad I am you came!"

The girls filled the hall with excited chatter as they pulled off their boots and jackets.

Pulling Grace with her, Nora dashed down the hall toward her study. "Alec, it's not the police! Call them quickly!"

The Best Friends gasped in alarm. "The police?" they all said at once.

"I'll explain," Kathy said. "Come with me." She hurried to the study. Diane wasn't with Alec. She had apparently gone up to warn Aaron Bellwood. "Come on!" Kathy raced down the hall and up the stairs with the Best Friends behind her. She found Diane in the second-story hallway. Her face was white and her eyes full of fear.

Diane grabbed Kathy's hand. "He's gone!"

"Gone?" Kathy pulled away and dashed into the bedroom where Aaron had been. "But he's sick!"

"What's going on?" Chelsea caught Kathy's arm.

As quickly as she could, Kathy told the story while Diane ran downstairs to tell Nora and Alec. Diane returned just as Kathy said, "We have to find him!"

"Did you look through the other rooms?" Hannah asked in a calm, businesslike voice.

"Not yet." Diane shook her head.

"Let's each take a room and look." Hannah quickly assigned the girls to the various rooms. They split up and ran to the different rooms. In a short time they were back with the report that he wasn't in any of them.

Diane's heart sank. "Let's check the other wing." She led the way. Once again they split up and looked, then met back in the living room and stood in a tight group in the middle of the large room.

"Why would he leave?" Diane nervously rubbed her hands up and down her sleeves.

"Maybe he heard your folks were going to call the police," Kathy said.

"Maybe." For once Diane didn't correct Kathy for using the word "folks."

Hannah frowned thoughtfully. "You said he didn't look like a street person because he looked too clean and well dressed."

They all turned to listen to Hannah.

"That means he didn't wear only the one change of clothes for the entire time he's been in and out of the house. Where did he keep his clothes? His shaving kit? All his stuff?"

"Yeah, where?" Roxie asked.

"That's what we have to find out. Here's what we'll do." Hannah talked for a few minutes, then split them into two teams—herself, Diane, and Roxie on one, Chelsea and Kathy on the other. She thought it was wise to put Kathy and Roxie on different teams because they still occasionally fought about Roy Marks. "Look for details—a water spot on the floor, whiskers in a sink, soap scum in a tub, fingerprints on the walls or woodwork. There could be a hidden closet or even a hidden room. Meet back here in ten minutes."

"What about in the woods?" Kathy looked out the window toward the trees where they'd seen Aaron Bellwood. "Could there be a cabin in the woods?"

They all looked at Diane for the answer.

She shrugged. "If there is, we never heard about it."

"Or even a treehouse," Chelsea said.

"We'll check out the woods after we search the house." Hannah burst out laughing. "This is fun!"

126

"It's sure a different way to spend a Sunday afternoon." Kathy looked at her watch. "It's really late! It'll be dark soon. We'd better look outdoors first."

"Good idea," they all agreed.

Diane turned to Kathy. "How about praying that we'll find Aaron Bellwood quickly? And that he's safe."

Kathy smiled warmly at Diane. "Sure." She bowed her head with the others and prayed.

Her eyes filling with tears, Diane listened to Kathy pray and even prayed under her breath. How wonderful it was to know again that God cared!

A few minutes later Diane led the way downstairs. She found Nora and Alec in the kitchen with Grace, having tea. "Aaron Bellwood's not upstairs, so we're going to look in the woods."

Alec nodded. "We looked in all the rooms downstairs, and I checked the barn too. He's not here."

Nora set her cup down. "We got ahold of the police in time to stop them from coming."

Diane sighed in relief.

Grace pushed her cup back. "We've been trying to figure out a way to find his family so we can let them know he's still alive."

"Abe Parker knew them," Kathy said as she pulled on her boots and jacket. "He told us yesterday when we cleaned his basement."

"I'll call him!" Grace reached for the phone book that lay on the table between her and Nora.

Kathy forced back a flush. Would Ty be with his grandpa? He said he'd ask him where the Bellwoods lived.

Diane pulled her hat over her head as she watched the Best Friends head for the back door. They really didn't need to help, yet they were glad to do so. She followed them out and shivered. The temperature had dropped. She pulled on her mittens.

"What are you doing?" Stuart called from the driveway as he and Elaine ran toward them.

Kathy quickly explained. "Want to go with us?"

"Sure!" Elaine's cheeks and the tip of her nose were red with cold. "We finished our chores already."

Roxie looked longingly toward the barn. "I sure would like to see the horses."

"Later," Hannah said. "Lead the way, Diane."

She nodded and ran toward the woods.

Stuart fell into step beside Diane. "Watch for footprints."

"I will." She liked Stuart, and that surprised her. She'd been all set to hate both him and Elaine. Once again it had been Kathy who'd changed her mind. As soon as she could, she'd talk to Kathy again about God and His love. But right now she had to concentrate on the ground in the woods so she wouldn't miss a thing. Twigs snapped as the others ran behind her. Up ahead she heard a blue jay cry out.

Suddenly Diane stopped. The others almost ran into her. She pointed to the ground in a clearing a few feet away. The trees were far enough apart that the ground had been covered with snow. In that snow they could see three clear footprints and a smudged one.

"Footprints big enough to be a man's!" Stuart whispered.

Diane flushed with pride. She'd found the footprints. But were they Aaron Bellwood's? She turned to the others. "We have to be very quiet just in case he's nearby. We don't want to frighten him."

They all nodded in agreement.

Slowly they walked across the clearing in the direction of the footprints and into the woods. They hesitated. Elaine pointed out scattered leaves, so they went that way.

A few minutes later Kathy caught sight of what looked like the edge of a roof. Her pulse leaped, and she suddenly felt too hot inside her jacket and boots. "Look!" she whispered, pointing to a cluster of trees.

"What do you see?" Chelsea peered in the direction Kathy was pointing. Chelsea saw two trees without leaves, two pines with sweeping boughs, and some oaks with brown leaves that rustled in the wind like paper.

Kathy pulled off her cap and let the wind blow through her blonde curls. "I thought it was a cabin. Maybe it's nothing," she said lamely.

"Let's look." Diane lifted her arm high. "Come on!" With her heart lodged in her throat, she led the way toward what Kathy thought was a cabin. Maybe they'd find Aaron Bellwood there.

Diane stopped between the oaks and looked. A fallen tree leaned against the maples. "No cabin," she said in disappointment.

"Sorry." Kathy flushed.

"Hey, it's better to check everything." Chelsea patted Kathy's arm. "We'll keep looking."

"God is with us," Diane said softly.

"That's right!" they all agreed.

Diane smiled as she led the way deeper into the woods. And a few minutes later she did spot a cabin—no mistake this time. It was small, with two windows and a door. The logs had weathered, and the cabin blended in with the surrounding area. Her mouth turned bone-dry as she stopped the others and pointed. She couldn't speak. She'd thought there wouldn't be a cabin. She'd thought they might not find Aaron Bellwood. But now . . .

"We have to be very quiet," Kathy whispered. "Come on, Diane." Kathy slipped her arm through Diane's, and they led the way to the door of the cabin.

The door was open, and Aaron Bellwood stood inside with his luggage on the floor beside him. He looked tired.

"Why'd you leave?" Diane asked from the doorway.

Aaron jumped, then faced them. "I was causing too much trouble. I figured if my family didn't care enough about me to leave word where they were moving, I didn't care either."

"They thought you were dead," Stuart said. "I was a little boy when they moved, but I remember."

Aaron brushed a tear from his eye. "Did they tell your folks where they were going?"

Stuart frowned thoughtfully. "I think they were going to see their children, but that's all I remember."

Diane stepped into the cabin. It had one room and was clean and tidy but cold. "Come back to the house."

"We want to help you." Kathy smiled. "My mom is trying to find your family."

Aaron took a deep, ragged breath. "I don't know . . ."

They all talked at once, trying to convince him to go with them.

He looked at Diane. "What about your parents . . . your dad especially? He wasn't happy about me being there."

"He changed his mind because I said I wanted to help you." Diane looked beseechingly into Aaron's face. "Please go back with us. We do want to help you—we really do." She needed to help him get back with his parents! She couldn't be with hers until she got to Heaven, but he could. "Please?"

Aaron hesitated a long time, then smiled. "All right. I'll come with you."

The others cheered, filling the woods with their glad cry.

Diane squeezed Aaron's hand and smiled through her tears.

13

Aaron's Story

Back at the house, Aaron took a deep breath, then began to tell them all his story. Remembering was hard, and talking about it was even harder, but his new friends seemed to really care, and that made it easier for him to tell them his story.

■

His heart thundering, Aaron looked in the mirror. An hour ago at the mall he'd had his ear pierced. Glen Spears had laughed in delight and said it looked great. It had taken Glen about six months to convince Aaron to have it done. Aaron frowned. Now at home the earring seemed to be as big as his entire head. Maybe he should take it out and throw it away. Mom had said he absolutely could not have his ear pierced, no matter how many of his friends did. He shouldn't have listened to Glen.

Groaning, Aaron turned away from the mirror. Why couldn't he find the backbone to stand against Glen and his ideas? Aaron sank to the chair at his desk. Piles of clothes dotted the floor. His bedspread lay halfway on the floor. The wastebasket overflowed with papers from trying to get his English paper written. At least the house was silent for once. Usually it rang with noise from his twin brothers Terry and Jason and his sister Bonny. They were in college and often brought friends home. He liked listening to them and laughing at their antics, but they almost always sent him away because he was only fifteen and in the way. He hated their thinking he was in the way! He loved them with his whole heart, but they thought he was a baby and pushed him away.

Today they'd be home for his birthday dinner. He was sixteen—finally old enough to hang out with them. Tomorrow he'd get his driver's license. He gingerly touched his ear. They'd all hate his earring, just like they hated the way he dressed and the friends he hung out with. But even when he'd tried to be and do what they wanted, they still didn't include him.

Just then someone knocked on his door. "Aaron, can I come in?"

It was Mom! He thought about yanking the earring out or hiding it from her. But he wouldn't do either! He took a deep breath. His palms were damp with sweat. "Come in, Mom."

She sailed in, all smiles. "Wait'll you see your cake! I just finished decorating it. It has . . ." She stopped mid-sentence when she spotted his earring, and the smile left her face. Tears welled up in her eyes. "Aaron! Aaron, what have you done?"

His legs trembled. If only he could rip out the earring and fill in the hole! He lifted his chin. "I got an earring. What's wrong with that? Everybody has one."

"I suppose if everybody jumped off a cliff you'd do it too."

"Same old line, Mom. Can't you come up with a new one?"

"Aaron, it's not the earring I'm upset about, and you know it! It's your deliberately doing the things your dad and I tell you not to do." She reached out for him, but he stepped out of her reach. Pain crossed her face. "I love you, Aaron. I only want the best for you."

"This earring is best! Being friends with Glen Spears is best!"

"Stop it!" Fire flashed from Mom's blue eyes. "Glen is not a Christian, and you know it. He lies and cheats and drinks!"

"Who says he does?" Aaron shouted. "Sure, Terry said so, but why do you believe him over me?"

"Your brother knows what he knows." Mom gripped the back of the chair. "I want you to take the earring out and leave it out."

"No."

She trembled. "You take it out or I will!"

He shook his head. His heart thundered, and he

backed further away from her so she couldn't hear the telltale heartbeat.

She took a deep, steadying breath. "Take out the earring and come on downstairs for your birthday dinner. Let's make it a nice evening to remember."

He stood in silence as she walked out. He reached to take out the earring, then stopped. Why should he? He was his own person, wasn't he?

Slowly he brushed his hair back into a ponytail and wrapped a band around it to hold it in place. He touched his T-shirt that said PLAY HARD, LIFE IS SHORT. He knew Dad hated it, but he'd wear it anyway. What else was new? Mom and Dad hated everything about him.

He walked down the long hall to the stairs. He loved this house. It was big and beautiful with more rooms than they used. Someday he'd like to own the house and raise a family in it. He grinned. Wouldn't Dad get a hoot out of that? Dad thought Aaron hated everything about Bellwood Estate. But he didn't. He loved it and was proud it was his home.

Laughter drifted out from the kitchen where they were all working together to get the meal on. The aroma of stuffed cabbage made his mouth water. It was his favorite, and that's why Mom had made it. Tonight they were eating in the big dining room. Grandma and Grandpa were coming, along with a few cousins and aunts and uncles. All of them had brought a dish to pass. Aunt Colleen had probably brought the corn casserole that nobody liked except her and Uncle Butch.

Aaron stopped in the hall outside the kitchen. It wasn't too late to take out the earring and change the shirt. Should he? In his mind he heard Glen laughing at him, telling him he was a wimp because he always did what his folks wanted. Well, he wasn't a wimp!

He walked silently into the kitchen and stood near the door. The kitchen was full of people—some at the table playing a game and others at the island counter. The birthday cake stood on the utility cart in all its splendor. It was decorated like a soccer field with all the players in place. Eight candles stood behind each goal. Soccer was his favorite sport, and he was good at it. Yesterday he'd quit the team, but he hadn't told his family. He'd quit because Glen had said soccer kept him too tied down.

Finally Grandma noticed Aaron. She rushed over to him and hugged and kissed him. "Happy birthday, sweetheart!"

"Thanks." Her eyes let him know when she spotted his earring and read his shirt, but she didn't say anything. He was glad.

He didn't know how he made it through the night, but he managed to. It was hard to look at Mom. He could tell she was close to tears. Dad was close to exploding with anger, but he kept it in check until everyone had gone home.

"Get into my study!" Dad gripped Aaron's arm

and forced him down the hallway. Seconds later they stood inside, toe to toe. Already Aaron was the same height, but Dad outweighed him by about fifty pounds. "Aaron, I will not tolerate a rebellious spirit in my house!"

"I'm not being rebellious just because I like things different from you." But he knew he *was* being rebellious—he just couldn't help it. He tried not to be, but he was anyway.

"The earring and the shirt are small things, son. We both know that. But it's much deeper."

Aaron blocked out the speech he'd heard a million times in the past six months. At long last Dad let him go to bed. He carried up his gifts and dropped them in a heap on his floor. Couldn't anyone think of something besides clothes to give him? He touched the twenty dollar bill in his pocket. Aunt Betty had given him that. She was probably sorry she had after she'd seen his earring.

He sprawled across his bed and fell asleep with his clothes on.

For the next few months he did his best to stay out of Mom's and Dad's way so he didn't have to hear any lectures. Glen had convinced him to try drugs with him, and he did marijuana for a while, then quit. His grades slipped, but he didn't care. So what if he didn't go to college? He wasn't like the twins and Bonny. He was his own person! If he didn't want college, he wasn't about to be forced to go. Why should he do what the rest of the family did? He was Aaron Bellwood, not a clone!

He knew his mom and dad were praying for him, but he refused to think about that. On Sundays he pretended to be sick so he wouldn't have to go to church or he said he'd go with Glen. But they never went. Glen's parents didn't care.

Just before his seventeenth birthday he quit his part-time job so he'd have more time to go out with Angela and to party with Glen and his friends.

About a week before his birthday Mom stopped him at the back door. "Are you bringing Angela home tonight to meet us?"

"No." Aaron had learned early on not to argue. He reached for the door.

Mom caught his arm. "Aaron, are you sure she's a Christian?"

"Sure, Mom. I wouldn't go with her if she wasn't." The lie didn't bother him a bit. He'd gotten used to lying. When he was little Mom could always tell when he lied, but no longer. He'd gotten so he wouldn't bat an eye over it.

"Bonny said her friend Brenda saw Angela coming out of an X-rated movie last night. She barely had anything on, and she was hanging all over the man who was with her. Brenda said she looked like a hooker."

Aaron shrugged. He knew what she was, but he wasn't about to let Mom know. Mom had no idea he'd often gone to R- or X-rated movies. He liked watching them—why shouldn't he go? "Brenda probably saw somebody who looked like Angela."

Mom shook her head. "No, Aaron. It was Angela. You and I both know it." Tears welled up in Mom's eyes. "What has happened to you, son? Why are you making life so hard on yourself? You're putting yourself in Satan's territory. Please don't do it! You know Jesus loves you. His way is always the best way."

Aaron reached for the door again.

Again Mom stopped him. "I've decided to send you away to a Christian school. Your dad isn't totally for it, but he said if I think it'll help, we'll do it. You're going next week. It's all arranged."

Aaron's temper shot through the roof. Sending him away! And to a Christian school? "No way, Mom! I'm not going to a Christian school now or ever!"

"You're going," Mom said firmly. "It's settled."

"It's not settled with me! I will not go. You hear me? This is my home, and I'm staying right here!"

Mom's eyes flashed. "Oh, no, you're not! If we have to tie you up and drag you to that school, you're going! Aaron, the campus is nice. A lot of missionary kids attend the school. I've already looked at the dorm where you'll live. The standards are high, just like we want them to be."

Aaron's head spun, and he was so angry he could

barely see. "What makes you think you can make me go?"

"Because you're sixteen and under our care."

"Not for long!" he shouted.

That night he packed a few things and stayed the night with Glen. The next day he drove his car to Illinois, sold it and bought a cheaper one, and drove south until he felt like stopping. He sold the car in Missouri and bought a bus ticket to Dallas, Texas. He could easily get lost in Dallas. His anger kept him there even when he cried with loneliness and fear.

On his twentieth birthday and after a dozen low-paying, back-breaking jobs he decided it was time to finish high school and take a few college classes. He even considered calling his family, but he was too stubborn and still too angry. Many times he missed living in his beautiful house and walking in the woods at Bellwood Estate. At times he even missed the twins and Bonny. And Dad. He wouldn't let himself miss Mom. It was her fault he'd been forced to leave.

Just after he turned twenty-five he got married to Carlene Evans. They were deeply in love. She was short and slight with long wavy brown hair and bright blue eyes. They worked in the same company doing computer programing.

On their first anniversary Carlene slipped her arms around Aaron and looked up into his face. "Honey, you promised you'd call your family and tell them we're married. It's been a year!"

"I know. But it's been eight years since I left. That's too many years."

"I want to know them. You know *my* family. They love you, and you love them."

He nodded. He'd long ago given up his earring and had his hair cut short. At times he'd even thought about going to church. Once he'd bought a Bible to read. So far he hadn't opened it, but from time to time a Scripture verse would pop into his head. He'd thought he'd forgotten everything he'd learned, but he hadn't. Mom would be glad to know that. He pushed the thought aside.

"Aaron, I want to share my news with them."

"What news?"

With tears glistening in her eyes, Carlene smiled. "We're going to have a baby."

He picked her up and swung her around the room, then kissed her as if he'd never quit. "Our very own baby!" Suddenly he could see Bellwood Estate with all the rooms. He could see himself and Carlene with their baby in the house. He sank to the couch with Carlene on his lap. Why think about Bellwood Estate? He'd never take Carlene there, no matter how badly he wanted to.

"What's wrong, Aaron?" Carlene kissed his cheek. "Don't get depressed again."

"I won't." He forced the depression away—something that had dogged him for the past five years.

"Let's talk about names. Shall we name him Aaron Junior or Carlene Junior—if it's a girl?"

They had a boy and named him Garrett. Two years later they had a girl and named her Ellen.

When Ellen was three years old Carlene said, "Aaron, we can't raise these kids outside of church. Starting next Sunday, let's go as a family."

"Let's do it!" Aaron lifted Ellen and Garrett onto his lap. "You'll get to go to Sunday school class. Won't that be fun?"

"Yes!" Ellen cried, clapping her hands.

"No," Garrett snapped. "Sunday school is for sissies. Mark said so." Mark lived across the street from them and was Garrett's best friend.

"What does Mark know?" Aaron laughed and kissed Garrett's cheek. "We'll ask him to go with us."

"Okay." Garrett smiled. "If Mark'll go, then so will I."

The first Sunday in church Aaron and Carlene both rededicated themselves to the Lord. They vowed to God and each other that they'd raise their kids to know and love Jesus.

A month later Aaron tried to call his parents. There was no answer. He hung up, his body soaked in sweat. He didn't try again, even though Carlene begged him to.

Just after Garrett's fourteenth birthday he marched into the living room after spending the day with Mark at the mall. Garrett stopped in front of the

TV so Aaron and Carlene would see him. "I got my ear pierced today."

They gasped. Aaron was flung back in time when he'd done the very same thing—only he'd tried to keep quiet about it. Garrett was much bolder. Aaron forced himself to stay calm. He knew Garrett had done it out of rebellion. Shouting at him wouldn't help. Carlene started to jump up, but Aaron gave her a look that said to be patient.

"Well?" Garrett pointed to his ear.

"Be sure to put the medication on it so it won't get infected," Aaron said. Inside he was seething. He wanted to rip the earring out of Garrett's ear, then send him to his room for the rest of his life.

Aaron lost the next battle. Garrett had announced he would no longer go to church with them—Mark had quit three years ago, and now he would stop too. Aaron yelled at Garrett and grounded him for a month. Garrett did go to church with them, but he was always sulky when they went.

All the memories flooded back, and Aaron paced the bedroom floor. The pain he felt as a parent was much worse than the pain he'd felt as a teenager who'd walked away from home. What had he done to his mom and dad? He'd broken their hearts when all they wanted was whatever was good for him! What a fool he'd been! But no longer.

"Forgive me, Heavenly Father! Forgive me!" He wept giant tears that soaked his face and his shirt.

Later he tried to call them, but the phone number was no longer in service. He turned to Carlene who waited beside him, her eyes watchful. "That's not their number anymore. I'm going to go see them. Can you handle everything for a while?"

"Yes. You have a month of vacation time coming. Take it all if you need to."

"Thank you!" He kissed her and held her for a long time. "I'll tell the kids. If you have any problems with them, see if your mom will come for a while."

"I will. But they'll be fine."

Aaron flew to Grand Rapids, then rented a car. He drove to Bellwood Estate and let himself in the back door with the key he'd kept all those years. The furniture was different, but the house was the same— big and beautiful and peaceful. Slowly he came to realize his family didn't live there any longer. He left the house and decided to stay in the cabin in the woods the twins had built during their last year of college just before he left home. He parked the car in a secluded spot near the cabin, then daily walked to his house, each day hoping he'd find his parents. More and more he felt disoriented. Several times he slept in his old bedroom and thought he was still a teenager. Then he lost his key and got sick. He fell at the back door and hit his head. When he came to, two girls were leaning over him and he was lying on the kitchen floor. They fed him and took care of him. Somehow he got upstairs in Terry's old bedroom. He knew he couldn't stay there. Somehow along the way, his brain cleared, and he realized he was trespassing in a house that belonged to strangers. He sneaked back to the cabin to pack and go home.

"I couldn't find my parents, and maybe I never will," he said with a catch in his voice.

The Answers

Diane's eyes filled with tears as Aaron Bellwood finished his story. Darkness had fallen outdoors, but the lamps in the living room glowed softly. A fire crackled in the stone fireplace. She sat in the chair she'd started calling hers. The Best Friends sat nearby on the floor. They were wiping their eyes, and she knew they were crying too. Stuart and Elaine's dad had called them home before Aaron began his story.

Alec clamped a hand on Aaron's shoulder. "We'll do all we can to help you find your family. They sold this place to Jake Andrews, and he sold it to us. We already tried to get your parents' address from Mr. Andrews, but he said he doesn't have it."

"Sometimes I think God's punishing me for running away from home," Aaron said in a husky voice.

Diane held her breath and waited to see if anyone had an answer for that.

Grace Aber shook her head. "When you repented of your sins, Jesus immediately forgave you.

God doesn't punish you for something Jesus forgave. God loves you and wants the best for you."

"You punished yourself enough," Nora said. "Disobedience and rebellion put you in Satan's territory where he can do his evil to you. But you can stop him. He's defeated, and he can't harm you if you stand against him with Christ's help."

Diane's heart leaped. Kathy had said the same thing! Diane listened with interest as Nora, Alec, and Grace quoted verses from the Bible to show Aaron that God loved him and wanted the best for him even though he'd sinned. Silently Diane asked Jesus to forgive her for lying. And she prayed for help so she wouldn't lie again.

Nora touched Aaron's shoulder. "Aaron, one more thing—it's important to forgive yourself."

"I don't know if I can," he whispered.

Grace smiled. "Jesus said to, so you can—with His help."

Diane's heart leaped. She could forgive herself too! She no longer had to carry the guilt she felt for lying to Mommy and Daddy—nor the guilt she felt because they were killed and she wasn't. Silently she forgave herself. She knew the guilt was gone! She was free! She wanted to hug everyone in sight, but she sat quietly and listened to the adults as they talked. The Best Friends sat quietly and listened too.

Later Diane sat on the couch beside Aaron. She wanted to say something to him, even if the others heard. "Don't be afraid to talk to your mom and dad. You know they love you. If I could, I'd talk to mine and tell them how sorry I am for telling them a lie." She brushed a tear away. "I'd tell them I love them and miss them." Her voice broke, but she continued. "I know they're happy in Heaven, and someday I'll see them, but I wish I could see them now. I can't. But you can see yours." She brushed another tear away. "Find them and tell them how you feel or you'll be sorry for the rest of your life."

With tears sparkling in his eyes, Aaron took Diane's hand and kissed her cheek. "Thank you. I *will* try to find them."

Just then the front doorbell rang. A buzz of speculation on who it was filled the room while Alec hurried to the door. It was Abe Parker and Ty Wilton.

Kathy smiled, and Chelsea, Roxie, and Hannah frowned.

Smiling, Diane hurried over to Ty. "What did you find out?" she asked in a low voice.

"My Uncle Dan might know." Ty looked past Diane at Kathy and smiled.

Grace stepped forward and greeted them, then introduced Abe Parker to the others as she motioned for him to sit in a big overstuffed chair beside her.

Ty hurried to Kathy and sat down beside her. "I brought him. He says Uncle Dan might know where they are. He's going to give Aaron Bellwood the number and let him call."

"Good," Kathy whispered.

Diane took her chair again and locked her hands together as she listened to Abe telling them just what Ty had already whispered to Kathy.

"You can call from my study for privacy," Nora said.

Aaron shook his head. "I need all of you here for support."

Diane sighed in relief. She wanted to hear everything, and she knew the others did too.

Alec gave Aaron the cordless phone, and Abe Parker told him the phone number.

Aaron started to dial, then stopped. "Could we pray first, Alec?"

"Sure." Alec bowed his head and prayed for courage for Aaron and that he'd find his family and get back together with them.

Frowning, Ty nudged Kathy and whispered, "Does he really think praying will help?"

Kathy frowned at Ty. "Of course! God answers prayer."

Ty closed his mouth and didn't say another word, but he squirmed uncomfortably.

Diane locked her hands together in her lap as Aaron punched the number. Wood snapped in the fireplace, and she jumped. She felt the tension from the others as they waited in silence.

Aaron's mouth felt bone-dry. His hand was sweaty and slippery on the phone. When a man answered Aaron said, "This is Aaron Bellwood speaking. I'm looking for my parents."

"I'll be! This is Dan Parker. Me and your dad were great friends. I lost track of them about three years ago. They lived in Texas . . . Dallas, Texas."

Aaron almost dropped the phone. "That's where I live! Could they still be there?"

"I have their last address and phone number. Wait a minute, and I'll get them."

While he waited, Aaron told the others what Dan Parker had said. "He's getting the phone number and their last address."

"Here's a paper and pencil . . ." Grace pulled them from her purse and held them out to Aaron.

Smiling, he took them and wrote down what Dan Parker said. "Thanks for your help."

"Give them my best when you talk to them. They'll be mighty pleased to hear from you."

"Do you think so?"

"I know so. They prayed constantly for you. They hired a private detective to find you, but he couldn't. Finally they had to let him go."

Aaron's eyes filled with tears. "Thank you. I appreciate your help."

"I'm just glad you're going to find them. I've been praying for you too."

"You have?"

"Sure. You have my name, you know—your middle name Daniel is from me."

"I'd forgotten about that. Thanks again."

Aaron hung up and told the others what Dan had said. "I'd forgotten I was named after Dan Parker. When I needed a name to call myself when Kathy and Diane asked who I was, I took part of my middle name and part of my last name. That's how I came up with Dan Woods." He looked around the room. "I'm sorry for the trouble I caused. I thank you for all of your help."

"Aren't you going to try the number my son gave you?" Abe Parker asked sharply.

Aaron rubbed an unsteady hand across his forehead. "I don't know if I can."

"You can!" Diane cried, and the others agreed.

"If you say so." Aaron took a deep breath and punched the number. His hand shook so badly, he had to start over again. Before it rang, a canned recording came on saying the number was no longer in service. Aaron slowly hung up and gripped the cordless phone with both hands. "It's no longer in service," he whispered.

Diane sank back with a moan.

Alec tapped Aaron's arm. "We're not giving up! God answers prayer! We'll think of something else."

"That's right," Nora said.

Ty nudged Kathy. "I knew it wouldn't do any good to pray," he whispered.

Kathy pushed her face right up to his. "God always answers! You wait and see!"

"You're weird." Ty jumped up. "Ready to go, Grandpa?"

Abe Parker pushed himself up. "Let me know the outcome, will you?" He shook hands all around and walked out with Ty leading the way.

Several minutes later, after many suggestions on what to do next to find the Bellwoods, Grace stood up. "We have to get home, girls."

They groaned. They wanted to find the Bellwoods that very night.

Grace hugged Nora. "Don't forget all I said."

"I won't."

The Best Friends said good night to everyone, told Diane they'd be talking to her soon, and walked outdoors. A cold wind blew against them. Grace started the car, but it took a while for it to warm up. The snow plow had gone through, so the road was clear.

Suddenly Kathy sat bolt upright. "I have it, Mom!"

"What?" Grace asked.

"What?" Hannah, Roxie, and Chelsea asked.

"See if Ralph Gentry will interview Aaron on his TV show! Dad could talk him into it!"

Grace laughed excitedly. "That's a wonderful idea! We'll talk to him when we get home! They have a live show on Wednesday, and they might be able to do something."

Smiling, Kathy settled back, watched the lights of

Middle Lake appear, and listened to the others talk about her idea.

■

At Bellwood Estate Diane sat at the kitchen table with Nora and Alec. They were having a bowl of cereal before going to bed.

Nora finished hers first and pushed her bowl back, then propped her elbows on the table and studied Diane. "I had a long talk with Grace Aber about you. I wanted to know how to help you feel like part of the family—feel like a daughter."

Diane dropped her spoon in her bowl. "What did she say?"

"She said to treat you like a daughter." Nora grinned. "Doesn't that sound simple? Yet we weren't doing it. We didn't do anything for you when you lied to us. That was wrong! Parents don't let their kids get by with doing wrong. They punish them for it."

Alec nodded. "The Bible says a parent who doesn't discipline his child, hates his child. And we love you, Diane!"

Tears blurred Diane's vision. "Is that why you adopted me?"

Nora shook her head. "Alec, do you want to tell her?"

Grinning, he nodded. "We read the account about your parents being murdered. We read about you, and as we read, the Holy Spirit spoke to our hearts and told us to adopt you."

"We've been trying ever since that time. It took this long for the courts to allow us to adopt you." Nora reached over and squeezed Diane's hand. "God loves you so much that He told us to adopt you. Then He led us to buy this place so you'd have a wonderful place to grow up."

Tears spilled down Diane's cheeks. "I was so wrong about God! He really really does love me!"

Nora brushed tears from her eyes. "And so do we."

"From now on we're going to be parents to you, not just adults living on the fringe of your life." Alec brushed tears from his eyes. "I wanted you to have everything nice, especially in your room. But tonight I'm taking the TV out of your room. From now on when we watch TV, it'll be a family activity—something we do together. The three of us will have more time together. You shouldn't spend every waking minute by yourself in your room."

Diane smiled. She'd been sooo lonely!

Nora smiled. "I talked to Donna and Cal Black this afternoon. We said they could continue to board and train horses here. We asked them to teach you all about horses. They were pleased to agree. They want you to be friends with Stuart and Elaine. We want that too."

Diane swallowed hard. "Stuart and Elaine might not want me."

"They will," Alec said. "You're a great girl."

Diane picked nervously at her thumb. "I'm too fat to ride a horse."

Nora shook her head. "Do you think only thin people ride? Besides, you'll be losing your baby fat any day now. You'll see."

Diane's heart leaped.

Alec took Diane's hand in his. "Life won't always be wonderful, but we'll always *always* be here for you, just as you'll be here for us. We're a family—on happy days and on sad days. We're a family!"

"A family," Diane whispered around the lump in her throat.

■

Monday in school Ty rushed up to Kathy. "Well? Did you get your prayers answered?" He made the word *prayers* sound like a dirty word.

Kathy lifted her chin and smiled. "God always answers prayers. My dad got Aaron Bellwood on his TV show. Lots of people watch it, and if anyone knows where his parents are, they'll let him know."

Ty rolled his eyes. "I've been thinking about us, Kathy."

"There is no *us*!" She'd decided that yesterday. She would not put herself into Satan's territory so he could harm her! Going with an unsaved boy was totally against what the Bible said. She had known it all along, but now it was firm in her heart.

Ty leaned close to Kathy. "I don't want to go with a girl who's so religious."

"And I won't go with a boy who isn't a Christian."

Ty waved his hand as if to wave away the words. "So, anyway, we're not going together any longer. I know it'll break your heart, but that's the way it is."

Kathy laughed. "See ya, Ty. Hey, by the way I'm praying for you."

Ty flushed scarlet and hurried away.

Kathy looked around the hall for the Best Friends, then ran to tell them she was free of Ty. They'd be glad. That's how the Best Friends were.

◾

On Wednesday the Best Friends and Diane sat in Chelsea's basement watching the big-screen TV. Across the room Grace and Nora stood talking while they waited for Aaron Bellwood to be interviewed by Ralph Gentry.

"Diane, my dad has a surprise for you and your mom," Kathy whispered excitedly.

"And we know what it is," Hannah said smugly.

"We do." Roxie and Chelsea nodded and grinned.

Just then Alec Brewster, carrying his guitar, appeared on the screen. He played and sang.

Diane watched in awe. Nora cried out in shock, then stood listening with her hands on her heart. The Best Friends and Grace Aber had as much fun watching Diane and Nora as they did seeing Alec on TV. When Alec finished singing, Ralph Gentry introduced him, praised his singing, and then introduced Aaron Bellwood.

Diane caught Kathy's hand and held it tight as Aaron told his story. Immediately after the show he was flying back to Dallas to his family. He'd already said good-bye to everyone.

■

Two days later Aaron Bellwood called Diane at Bellwood Estates. "They called me, Diane."

Her heart leaped. "When will you see them?"

"This evening. Someone who knows them watched the show and called them, and then they called me. My twin brothers, their wives and children, my sister and her husband and children, and my mom and dad are coming. I called Kathy and her family and told them. But I wanted to tell you myself."

Diane wiped tears from her eyes. "I'm happy for you." They talked a while longer, then hung up. Diane ran from her room, down the hall to the stairs, and down to the ground floor. "Mom! Dad! Where are you? I have great news!"

■

As cold wind blew against her, Kathy dropped her bike outside Chelsea's garage and ran to the door. They were having a Best Friends meeting in Chelsea's special rec room, and she was already a little late.

Chelsea's little brother Mike opened the door, and Kathy called "Hi" as she ran past. Halfway down the stairs she shouted, "I've got great news! Wait'll you hear!"

The Best Friends ran to the bottom of the steps, their faces bright with expectancy.

Kathy jumped down the last two steps. Her eyes sparkled excitedly. She had news about Aaron Bellwood—news the Best Friends would be as excited about as she was because that's how best friends are.

"Aaron Bellwood found his family!" Kathy cried.

"We want to hear it all," Hannah said.

Chelsea nodded. "Every single detail."

"Tell us! Tell us!" Roxie caught Kathy's hand and led her to the pile of pillows on the floor where they always sat.

Kathy sank to a pillow and told the story—every bit of it.

You are invited to become a
Best Friends Member!

In becoming a member you'll receive a club membership card with your name on the front and a list of the Best Friends and their favorite Bible verses on the back along with a space for your favorite Scripture. You'll also receive a colorful, 2-inch, specially-made I'M A BEST FRIEND button and a write-up about the author, Hilda Stahl, with her autograph. As a bonus you'll get an occasional newsletter about the upcoming BEST FRIENDS books.

All you need to do is mail your NAME, ADDRESS (printed neatly, please), AGE and $3.00 (U.S. currency only) for postage and handling to:

BEST FRIENDS
P.O. Box 96
Freeport, MI 49325

WELCOME TO THE CLUB!